THE DARK MARSHES

England, late 1800s: Henrietta Marsh has felt a shadow following her for most of her life. There are whispers among her colleagues that this darkness led to the violent death of her parents. When she is incarcerated in a mental hospital, she charts the events that led her there. Meanwhile, her only friend, and the man she loves, fight to save her. But can Henrietta be trusted, or is she truly mad — and guilty of the heinous crimes of which she is suspected?

SALLY QUILFORD

THE DARK MARSHES

Complete and Unabridged

LINFORD
Leicester

First published in Great Britain in 2015

First Linford Edition
published 2016

A catalogue record for this book is available
from the British Library.

ISBN 978–1–4448–2913–6

Published by
F. A. Thorpe (Publishing)
Anstey, Leicestershire

Set by Words & Graphics Ltd.
Anstey, Leicestershire
Printed and bound in Great Britain by
T. J. International Ltd., Padstow, Cornwall

This book is printed on acid-free paper

1

Introduction by Nan Bradley

My name is Anne Bradley, but most people call me Nan. I was a maid at Marsholm Manor from the age of twelve, and I was the maid of Lady Henrietta Lakeham prior to her marriage. I've been asked to put together all the documents pertaining to the case involving Lady Henrietta Lakeham's incarceration in an insane asylum and the tragic events that followed.

I don't know why I've been chosen to do this, though I do appreciate His Grace's faith in me.

'You're a clever woman, Nan,' he told me, echoing something Mrs Marsh had said to me many years before when I first came up to Marsholm Manor from the Home Farm. 'You'll be able to make short work of this.' I'm not sure about that but I am happy His Grace thinks so.

The main problem with telling the story has been knowing where to start. The beginning would be a good place, if only I knew where the beginning was. I wasn't there for all of it, and may God forgive me for that. If I had been, I might have been able to put a stop to the tragedy. There's others, with more invested in this story, that feel the same. So many people, including me, knew or suspected the truth but said and did nothing. Others were just too far away to be able to help, and by the time they came back it was all too late. I could cry when I think about it. But never mind that. I've got to get on and let the truth be known, as painful as it is.

Personally I'd have liked to leave out the twitterings of the Misses Molly and Dolly Marsh. It seems to me those old ladies talk a load of rubbish, but I'm told that there's a lot of truth in their ramblings. I'm not sure I can see it myself, but there you go.

Not everyone has wanted to tell their side of the story, and that's their right, I suppose. Not all have been able to. They did not leave any documents — that we have found — to aid our inquiries.

Something tells me that the doctor's testimony is the right place to start, even though he didn't come in till very late in the story. But it does explain why Miss Hetty was at the asylum.

*From the notes of Dr Herbert Fielding
St Jude's Private Asylum*

The patient is of great interest to me. Several weeks ago she was brought in kicking and screaming — as many are to this establishment — by her stricken cousin, Miss Cora Marsh. I remember that dear lady's sad eyes even now, as she explained the situation to me.

'There will be a great scandal if anyone finds out she is here,' Miss Cora explained, her china-blue eyes large and terrified. 'So I beg you to keep it quiet, at least until my darling cousin is cured.'

'Have no fear,' I said, taking her hand, which trembled like a bird in mine. 'We have had royalty through these doors and no one has ever known.' I was tempted to tell her how, as a young physician, I had treated members of the royal family. I felt sure it would impress her, but I was sworn to secrecy. Of course, others took credit for helping royalty, but I felt sure my treatment helped. If Miss Cora had known that, she might not consider me such a dry old stick.

'Thank you, Dr Fielding,' she said, squeezing my hand. 'The moment I met you, I knew that I could rely on you. The problem is, my cousin is under a rather strange delusion. Nothing we say can alter her belief that she has done this terrible thing.'

I am a great believer in the power of literature, and that man — or woman — most reveals himself when he keeps a journal. So I have suggested to the

4

patient that she write down the events that led her to this place. I suspect that Miss Cora has put her cousin here to protect her. I admire her loyalty, just as I admire her grace and beauty, but I intend to find out the truth about what happened.

Since arriving, after we had restrained and sedated her, the patient has shown all signs of regaining her equilibrium. She sits quietly in her room, looking out of the window. She submits to treatments without complaint, and she is polite to the staff. But I am mindful of the words of Miss Cora, as she left.

'Whatever you do,' she whispered to me, terror etched on her lovely face, 'don't trust her.'

Testimony of Henrietta Lakeham

' . . . and you will know the truth and the truth will make you free,' Dr Fielding said, as he looked at me over his spectacles. I think he means to be kind, but I have witnessed that his kindness is often cruel in its expression. Such as when he insisted on a succession of ice baths for poor Mrs Lillehammer, in order to cure her hysteria. Her illness had manifested itself in her falling in love with a man who was not her husband. As such, society has decreed that she must be very sick. Her husband, on the other hand, had kept another woman and seven illegitimate children for many years. As a result, he is considered to be a very healthy male indeed.

Then there is Olive, a maid to a great lady, who was sent here for insanity due to exhaustion. She tells me that she alone had to keep a fifteen-bedroom house in perfect condition, and this led to her collapsing in hysterics one day. Had she been a rich lady, she might have gone abroad or somewhere like Bath to take the waters. Here, the only water she has known involves hundreds of icy cold showers to cool her fevered mind.

So if I say that I write this only to avoid such treatments, you will perhaps understand.

It is bad enough to now be considered one of the Dark Marshes. For most of my life, my maiden aunts, Molly and Dolly, have told me tales of the Marshes: the medieval Marsh who joined the church and then persuaded his congregation that judgement day had come; the Civil War Marsh who had hung roundheads from the gate; and finally my father . . .

If not for my cousin Cora, I might have gone mad then. Six years older than I, she had lived with us since her own parents died. She became a sister to me. When Mother and Father died, she was the one who held me as I cried. She was also the one who told me the truth about my father, whilst others whispered about it behind my back.

When I was sent to live with Aunts Molly and Dolly in the old hunting lodge on our family estate, Cora came with me. The main house, Marsholm

Manor, was meant for the distant cousin who had inherited the estate. The lawyers could not persuade him to live in the house, and I must admit I was glad. I hated the thought of anyone taking over the home in which my parents had been happy. And they had been happy, regardless of what anyone said.

I hated the hunting lodge, too, with its dark corners and dead animals staring down from the walls. I was only ten years old, and the stuffed animals terrified me. I felt sure I heard them whispering and laughing at me as I passed by. Aunt Molly and Dolly hardly seemed to notice, whilst Cora would laugh affectionately and call me a silly goose.

Nan, who was eighteen at the time, came with us and for that I was grateful. Her common sense saw me through many dark moments. 'Those animals are dead,' she said to me as she tucked me in at night. 'As far as I know, animals don't have an afterlife, so they'd not be coming back as ghosts. There are evil things closer to home, Miss Hetty.'

'What do you mean?' I'd ask.

'Never mind. Just remember that I'm here if you want me, any time of the day or night.'

It was then, from Molly and Dolly, I learned about the insanity that runs in our family, leading to the murderous rages I have already described. As a result, I have tried always to be calm and benign, to the point that I am sure many people find me very dull indeed. It was Cora who brought joy and laughter into everyone's life, and I was content to remain in her shadow.

I believe that this story begins properly on the night I met him, because it is my love for him that has led me to the straits in which I find myself.

I was eighteen years old and had just come out. As a young heiress with a sizeable fortune, I was considered a good catch, even if not a very exciting one. I hated going out in public, as I already felt that people were judging me to be a Dark Marsh. As such, it made me reticent in my dealings with people.

'Come, dearest,' I remember Cora saying that night when we were invited to a ball at Colonel and Lady Markham's. 'It doesn't matter what the villagers whisper amongst themselves, or what those silly county girls say about you behind your back. You are not your parents.'

I am sure she did not mean to remind me of them; she was just being helpful. But as we set out for the ball, I began to play out those last few days before they met their end. By the time we reached the ball, I was a flurry of nerves. Molly and Dolly fluttering around, dressed in black and white like a couple of demon magpies, did not help.

'Straighten your dress, Hetty,' Molly said, pulling at my sleeves.

'Your hair is coming undone,' Dolly said, pulling at my curls.

'She will come undone in a moment if you don't stop,' said Cora, laughing. 'For goodness sake, dear aunts, leave her alone.' She put her arm through mine. 'Hetty, I hear that Sir George Lakeham is here tonight.'

'Who?' I asked.

'Dear child,' she said gently. 'You must remember me telling you about him. Mama and Papa used to know him in France, before they died. He is a close friend of royalty. Some say he will be given even greater honours in the future. Maybe even a dukedom. You must come and meet him.'

I wanted to do nothing of the sort. But neither did I want to appear rude. I excused myself and went to the powder room instead. I needed a few moments to cool my hot cheeks and calm my fluttering heart. I was not good in public, yet here I was, expected to play the gay debutante.

The powder room was in fact a small sitting room that had been set aside. A couple of the county girls were in there,

11

Jemima Harrison and . . . I forget the other girl's name now. They were whispering to each other. They stopped the moment I entered.

'Good evening,' I said, smiling politely.

'Hello, Hetty,' Jemima said. 'It is good to see you out and about.'

I almost told her that I knew from Cora that only the week before she had been gossiping about me.

'I'm having a party at my house next week, for my birthday,' said Jemima. 'Would you like to come?'

'I'll have to ask Cora what we're doing,' I said.

The girls looked at each other, and then nodded curtly before leaving me alone. No doubt they felt satisfied that they had dispensed with the niceties of inviting me.

The room had doors opening out onto a terrace. My aunts would have been horrified about me going out into the cold night — it was said there would be a frost — but for me the cold was welcome and did much to cool the heat of my brow.

I leaned on the bannister looking out to the garden. Above me, a full moon glowed. The trees had been decorated with coloured fairy lights, giving the garden a magical aura. Odd how I can still see it all. I have forgotten so many other things that have happened since then.

Perhaps it is because that was when I first saw him, walking among the trees. For a moment, I thought he was a spirit of the night, come to haunt me. Yet I was not afraid, despite his dark countenance and deep-set eyes. He stopped just a few feet away from me, and it seemed that we were both trapped in the spell.

'Hello,' he said.

'Hello,' I replied.

'Are you a nymph?'

'I am afraid not, sir. Are you a ghost?'

He laughed. 'Sometimes I wonder.'

'Whatever do you mean?'

'These events. I am not made for them.'

'I feel much the same way.'

'Oh you fit perfectly. A beautiful and fashionable young woman standing on the terrace. You could be Juliet waiting for her Romeo.'

'You are teasing me, sir.' I stood up straight, wanting to run away. Yet something prevented me from going. He moved closer and I got a good look at him. He was about twenty-two years old, tall and strong, with thick black hair. His eyes, in the dark, were midnight-blue and rimmed with jet black-lashes. I had never seen such a handsome man, and I immediately knew that he was out of my reach. Such men were not attracted to dull little creatures like me.

'No. I promise I am not.'

'You should see my cousin, Cora. She is the great beauty.'

'I am not interested in Cora. What is your name?'

'Henrietta Marsh.' I waited for a hint of recognition. Not of me, but of my infamous family name. I saw none.

14

He bowed in a courtly manner. 'I am very happy to meet you, Miss Marsh.'

'And your name, sir?'

'Hetty? Hetty, dearest, where are you?'

'I'm here, Cora. On the terrace.' I turned to see her.

'Who were you talking to?'

'A young man . . . ' I turned around but he was gone. 'He was there.'

Cora glanced out, then cast a doubtful look in my direction. 'I hope he was not being a nuisance, dear. Come along. Sir George is eager to meet you.'

I would be lying if I did not hope that the young man who spoke to me would turn out to be Sir George. It seems disloyal now to think such a thing.

Sir George certainly was handsome, but in a very different way. He was more than twenty years older than I for a start. That seemed ancient to me. Where the man in the garden had been dark, Sir George was fair. Where the man in the garden had been tall, Sir

George was of a more average height. He had dark lines under his eyes, suggesting he did not sleep much. He made every effort to be charming to me, but I am afraid I was an ungrateful recipient of his interest.

'Delighted, Miss Marsh,' Sir George said, and I believed he was, though what about I was not sure. 'Your cousin has been telling me of your kindness and nobility.'

'Cora always overstates my virtues,' I said.

'I am biased by my affection for you, my darling,' Cora said. 'But I do think you look very pretty tonight. What say you, Sir George?'

'I agree.' He bowed. 'Will you save a dance for me on your card, Miss Marsh?'

I suppose I must have agreed, because a few dances later, Sir George partnered me. He insisted on dancing with me again after that. Three dances later, I could see people talking. I would never have danced with a man that often, as it went against society's expectations, but Cora encouraged me and I felt she knew best.

'Don't let him go,' she whispered. 'He is already besotted with you.'

I did not believe that and told her so.

'Honestly, dearest, modesty is all very well, but don't let it become a fault.'

Whilst dancing with Sir George and my other partners, I looked for the stranger from the garden. Sometimes I thought I saw his reflection in the mirror, but when I looked again he was gone. Sometimes I wonder if I really did imagine him.

Where was I? Yes, dancing with Sir George. I did not dislike him. He was attentive enough, but a little too sure that he had won my hand. I felt I should demur a little more, but Cora would not hear of it.

'Dearest, you are a wonderful girl, but not as sparkling as the other debutantes,' she told me that night, as we talked under the covers. She often came into my bedroom to whisper in my ear, though Nan did not like it and would sometimes insist Cora go back to her own room so I could get some rest. 'You cannot let such a chance pass you by.'

'But I don't have to be married, Cora. I have enough money to live as a spinster. And what of you? Where will you go if I marry? Surely you don't want to stay with Molly and Dolly.'

'I have thought about that, and it occurs to me that I could live with you as a companion. All great ladies have them.'

That cheered me up immensely. 'Yes! That would be wonderful. I could not bear to be parted from you, Cora. You're the only person who understands me. But why does it have to be Sir George? I saw another young man in the garden. He was so handsome.'

'Oh, which of your partners was he?'

'None of them,' I confessed. 'I did not see him again.'

'Oh . . .'

'Oh what?'

'Nothing, dear. I'm sure he was very nice, but well, if he did not ask you to dance . . . '

'He was not interested in me. Is that what you are saying?'

'Perhaps he was already promised to someone else.'

'Yes, that is probably it.'

'So, you will accept Sir George's offer?' she almost pleaded with me.

'He has not offered yet!'

'I feel sure he will. He would be a fool not to. You are everything a man could want in a wife. Calm and serene. Well, until that temper of yours gets going.'

'I am not that bad, am I?' It was true I could become impatient at times. Sometimes I felt the darkness within me, but for the most part I managed to keep it in check.

She hugged me. 'No, of course not. But you did break that teacup yesterday because the tea was not to your liking, dearest.'

'I did not break it on purpose. It

slipped from my hand.'

'If you say so, dear.'

I turned away from her and thumped my pillow hard. 'I did not do it on purpose.'

'Darling, I'm so sorry.' She stroked my hair. 'I don't want to anger you again.'

I lay awake that night, thinking about the man in the garden and Sir George and the deepseated anger that I only just managed to control. The tea had been cold, but that was partly my fault as I had not wanted to come in from the garden. Nan had to call me several times.

I replayed the scene in my mind and eventually I had to concede that Cora was right; I probably had thrown the cup to the ground. Poor Nan. How she must have feared me and my outbursts. I am not surprised she chose to leave me when I married.

The shame of my behaviour towards a girl who has been a true friend engulfs me. I can write no more for crying.

From the notes of Dr Herbert Fielding

It is clear from reading the patient's own testimony that her neurosis began at a very young age. I am particularly interested in the whispering animals. It shows a very marked hysteria.

I do believe that this case could make my career, which has thus far been rather unexciting. If I could find out the secret of the Dark Marshes, and what's more, cure the most recent victim of the madness, I might even win a knighthood.

When Miss Cora came to visit her cousin, I was suitably discreet about the patient's journal, but I did, in my tactful way, bring up the subject of the man she met at the ball.

'Oh dear,' Miss Cora said, her lovely face forlorn and helpless. 'I had hoped she would stop talking about him.'

'Then you know him?'

'That's just it,' said Miss Cora. 'There is no man. The man of whom she speaks exists only in her imagination.'

It was just as I had thought.

2

Testimony of Molly and Dolly Marsh

To think that a Servant like Nan Bradley would have the Audacity to ask us to write down our account of the Tragedy that befell our Family. We want to make it Clear that if His Grace had not then visited to insist, we would Not do be Doing this at all. There was little Need for him to be so Brusque about it.

We are Christian women and speak Nothing but the Truth. Neither will we be Bullied into writing Separate Accounts. What, we ask, is the point? Molly and Dolly Marsh are never apart and we always speak as one. Whilst we may take it in turns to write parts of this Testimony — for our poor old hands do ache so on cold days — One Account is all they shall Receive.

We are the daughters of Sir Peregrine

Marsh and the sisters of Lady Henrietta's father, Julius Marsh, May God forgive him for his Wicked ways. For most of our Lives we lived at Marsholm Manor, the family home in Derbyshire.

Julius was Twenty years younger than us, from our father's Second Marriage to a Miss Dunfree. We still call her Miss Dunfree, because she died in childbirth, hardly having time to become our stepmother. God rest her Degenerate soul.

Father had Always wanted a Son, and Miss Dunfree left him Twin boys. We have been asked who was Born first. We were told it was Julius, and that Alexander was Born ten minutes Later. We were Not in the Room at the time, as it would not have been Fitting for Spinsters to be Present at the birth of a child, so we Do Not know that for Certain.

Despite what has been said About us, We were Happy to have Brothers, because at least it stopped our Home being Entailed away to some cousin, who we gather was Born in a Slum. It meant that We would Still have somewhere to Live when our Father died.

We were Fond of our Brothers, particularly Alexander, who was such a Spirited child. Julius was quieter, but we Distinctly remember the Madness in his eyes. Of course We did not Know how things would Turn Out, but Looking Back the Signs were there. When the Tragedy involving our Brother and his Wife took place, we said to Each Other It was Always going to Happen.

When Julius Married, not long after Father's death, we Stayed on at Marsholm Manor and we must Concede that Julius was always very Gracious to us. It Must be said that he Sometimes expressed Impatience with us — not that we Gave him Any Cause.

He married Miss Charlotte Portland, an Heiress in her own Right, with a Fifty Thousand Pound fortune. When they Married, he put all that Money into a Trust Fund. He said it was so that if they Only had Daughters, the young Ladies need not worry about their Future as we had worried about Ours until our Brothers were Born.

He left such a Strange last Will and Testament. The estate would, as was Custom, be given to the Next male in the Family line. This was a Distant Cousin whom We did not Meet for a very long Time. The money in the Trust Fund was left to Henrietta, with the Proviso that even when she Married, the Money remained Strictly under Her control. If she Died, then the money would go Directly to her Children, or in the Event of her having No children, back to the Marsholm Estate.

If you Ask us, It was Scandalous. A Woman should never be Responsible for that Much money, and a Wife should always Defer to her Husband in matters of Finance. We wonder that Sir George took an Interest in her at all. A Man needs to feel that he is the Master in his own Home.

Of course we expected to Marry, so we did not Expect Julius to Provide for us. We were not Unattractive as young Women, but neither did we want to be Separated, so Both of us Turned down Several Suitors. We Refused so many, that eventually they stopped Asking. Julius did leave us the Lodge in which to live and Five Hundred pounds a year each. One would have Hoped for more. But we were not Bitter, as some people have suggested!

Our other Brother Alexander joined the Army and we did not see him for Many years. He died Overseas, as did his Wife, and young Cora was brought to Marsholm Manor. Of course we took the Darling girl to our hearts. She was Ten Years Old but already a beauty, with such Nice manners. And how she loved her little cousin, Hetty — which was what she called Henrietta. Even though very Young herself, Cora Insisted on Helping the Governess to Care for Hetty.

We Believe it was Also around this time that Nan came to work at Marsholm Manor. We have No idea whence she Came, or how Old she was. We do Not concern Ourselves with the Details of Servants.

She was in the kitchens, but Succeeded in fooling Dear Julius and Charlotte into letting her Help to care for Hetty.

Nan was a Sullen girl, especially when Cora was Nearby. This was Undoubtedly because Cora was so Beautiful. We still remember her Golden curls and Cornflower-Blue eyes. Nan was pretty enough, we Suppose, in that Lower-Class way that tends towards fatness in middle age, but she would never be Fêted as a Beauty in society and I think she Hated Cora for that.

We don't say that the Maid was not Devoted to young Hetty, but it sometimes Seemed that she thought the child Belonged to her. If the Child so much as cried, Nan would Snatch her from dear Cora's arms and take her from the Room. We spoke to our Brother about it Several times, but he Refused to let the girl go.

'Nan's doing the job she's been employed to do,' was all he would Say, before Shutting his Study door on us. It was No good Speaking to our sister-in-law. She spent Much of her time in Bed with Megrims, only Rising to spend a couple of hours each Day with her Daughter. She did Not take as Much care of poor Cora as she Should have. We Weep to Think of the Loneliness that child must have Suffered but We did not Fail in our Christian duty to Make her feel a Part of the Family even where Others have Failed.

What must we Discuss now? Oh yes, the Dark Marshes. We have been Asked to clarify some of the Information about the instances of Insanity in the Family. Personally we see no Reason why we Should air the family Shame, but His Grace is insistent and as we now rely on his Charity to keep a Roof over our Heads, we have no Choice but to Comply.

We grew up on the Stories. Our Mother used to Love to tell them, especially on Cold, Dark nights. Mama had a Great sense of the Dramatic. We Disapproved of course, but One did Not argue with One's mama.

The girls used to Ask us About it, and whilst we Believed it was wrong to Fill their young Heads with such Tales, we also Believed it was our Duty to tell the Truth about the family History.

As Spinsters, we were used to People not Listening to us, so we Suppose it was Nice when we were asked for our family Expertise. To say we Embellished is a very Cruel charge indeed, but what can one Expect from a Girl like Nan Bradley?

The first to go Mad was Percival Marsh, way back in Henry VIII's time. He was a Parson of the Brimstone and Ashes ilk. Some say he had Catholic leanings, but of course the Marsh family are, and Always have been, good Protestants. It might Explain his Descent into Madness. Too Much Communion Wine. We have always Abstained from alcohol, Preferring to keep our bodies Pure for when we Meet our Maker.

Percival Marsh had a particularly Devoted congregation, whom he Persuaded to join a Community that lived within the grounds of Marsholm Manor. It was he who Built the moat and drawbridge, so that they could Cut themselves off Completely. The Happenings at the manor were of the most Profligate type.

Being good Christian ladies, we have No idea what that can Mean. It makes the Blood run cold just to Think about it, so we Try very Hard not to Think about it at All. Needless to say, we are Sure the events were very Depraved indeed.

They have All gone to Hell since Percival persuaded them to take their Lives, before taking his own. It is said that his Ghost haunts Marsholm Manor. We have Never heard it, but Hetty always felt a Presence. When they took her to the Asylum, we realised that it was her own Sick mind.

Then there was Sir Kenneth Marsh.

He lived during the Civil War, and was a staunch Royalist, which is as it Should be. When Roundheads came to the District, he had them all arrested and then put their heads on stakes all around the estate. We hear it was very Gruesome and set the Royalist cause back somewhat even if we Believe that the Roundheads deserved it.

We must not forget Father's brother, Uncle Horatio. He did not Kill or Maim anyone, thank goodness. He would Disappear from the dinner table, saying, 'I'm going to see Rodney.' Mother and father would Roll their eyes, and when we asked who Rodney was, they would reply, 'Rodney is no one.' We were not Permitted to ask any more.

Horatio used to say that he Wanted to Die in Rodney's arms. As it Happened, he was Crushed under a horse when coming back from the tavern one night. It seems, looking back, that Uncle Horatio's friend Rodney was purely Imaginary, just like Hetty's young man.

Things might have been Better there if Nan had not lied for her. We still do not Understand why Julius and Charlotte trusted a Serving girl.

We have been called to Dinner, so we will finish our Testimony at some Other time.

Testimony of Lady Henrietta Lakeham

The doctor wishes to know more of my stranger. I only saw him once again before my marriage. I wanted to buy ribbon for Cora's new bonnet, because the milliner had let her down badly, so Nan and I walked down to the village. I remember it being a beautiful spring day, with blossom on the trees, and there was a bustle of activity in the market square as farmers brought their livestock to sell.

I must have lost Nan at some point. She had seen her sister and asked if she might go and talk to her. I agreed, of course. Nan only had one afternoon off a week. Home Farm was some five miles from Marsholm Manor, so she could not always make the trip. Sometimes Papa allowed her a full day so that she could visit her parents.

I think now of the drudgery that must exist in the life of a serving girl and how condescending I must have seemed, in allowing her five minutes out of her whole lifetime to talk to a beloved sister. How selfish I was, thinking only of new bonnets. And then I could think only of him, so I was halfway home before I realised that Nan was not with me. Afterwards, because I lied for her, she lied for me, and it got her into so much trouble when the truth came out. It is no wonder she hates me now.

He was just about to get into a carriage when I saw him. I wanted to call his name, but I did not know what it was. He seemed to just catch sight of me as he climbed into the carriage, and he paused and stepped back down again.

'Miss Henrietta Marsh,' he said with a smile.

'It is a pleasure to see you again, sir,' I said. 'I wondered what had happened to you at the ball.' I think I might have blushed then. I could hear the reproach in my own voice because he had not asked me to dance. 'I mean, I am sure you had more important matters in hand.'

'Yes . . . yes, I suppose I did. But still, I apologise for not dancing with you. You seemed happy enough with Lakeham.'

'I . . . I was honoured that he took such an interest in me, of course. My cousin tells me that he is a very important man.'

'And does that matter to you, Miss Marsh? That a man is important?'

'No, not at all. What I mean is that I am such an inconsequential . . . ' I paused and laughed. 'No, I will not say it, or my cousin Cora will be angry with me. She tells me I am too fond of claiming modesty, though I am sure I do not do it on purpose.'

'I do not think so either. However, I do apologise for not dancing with you. It was a mistake on my part.'

'Perhaps we may dance some other time.' I blushed again at my own boldness. How could this man make me say things that I would not dare say to another? All I can say is that with him I felt different. I felt a freedom that was missing from my life. I believed I might say anything to him and be forgiven.

'Sadly not, Miss Marsh. I leave for the West Indies today.'

'Oh. Will you be away for long?'

'I intend to be away a very long time. There is nothing for me in Marsholm Cell. I had hoped there might be, but . . . Let's just say I am in no position to ask wealthy young ladies to dance.'

'I do not care,' I said. 'Truly, sir, I do not. If I gave you any impression that it mattered, then I owe you an apology. How shallow you must think me.'

'Oh, I think you have hidden depths, Miss Marsh,' he said.

'I do not even know your name,' I said. 'Might I know that before you leave forever?'

'I am . . . Max Parish. And no, you won't know my family name. We are not from around here. I am just visiting the area.'

'I see, Mr Parish. Well, I am glad to meet you anyway.' I held out my hand, which he took in his. He raised it to his lips, and I could feel the warmth through my lace glove. He held onto my hand for a long time.

'And I you, Henrietta.' His use of my first name was familiar, and yet I could not find it in me to be alarmed. 'I wish I could ask you to wait for me, but I do not know if I will ever return.'

'Then I am sorry that we will not know each other better, Mr Parish.'

'As am I. Promise me that you will take care of yourself.'

'I always try to. And if I don't, then my cousin and my aunts do.'

He nodded, and opened his mouth as if to say something, but appeared to change his mind. 'Farewell,' he said, climbing into the coach.

I do not know why I should have felt sadness at the departure of a man I barely knew. I could not say I was in love with him, only that I liked him much better than the man I eventually married.

I walked home with a sense of losing something — someone — very important, and it made me unhappy. As I have already said, I was halfway home before I realised I had left Nan behind.

There was great consternation when I arrived home without her; and when Nan returned five minutes later, Cora and my aunts were very irate with her.

'It is my fault,' I said. 'I met a young man that I knew. The one at the ball, Cora. You remember I told you about him?'

'Oh yes,' said Cora, her eyes filled with concern.

'I just wanted to talk to him alone.'

'Hetty!' Molly and Dolly chorused. 'What outrageous behaviour.'

'No, Nan was not far away, were you, Nan?'

'No, Miss Hetty,' said Nan.

'I asked her to stand apart for a short while, so that I could speak to him. Then we were separated by the crowds and I thought it best to come home.'

'So you saw this young man?' Cora asked Nan.

'Yes, Miss Cora,' Nan agreed. 'Of course I did.'

'I see . . . I see. Well, we will say no more of this, but in future, we expect you to take greater care of Miss Henrietta. Or you will be dismissed. Do you hear?'

'Yes, Miss Cora.'

'Hetty, darling, do not alarm us in such a way,' said Cora, putting her arms around me.

Testimony of Nan Bradley

It might be best if I explain my part in this. I remember the day well, and I remember Miss Henrietta telling me that I could go and speak to my sister, Meg. I'd not seen her since her marriage, and I wanted to congratulate her on the birth of her first child and my first nephew. I'd written to her, of course, but that's not the same as being able to embrace Meg and tell her how happy I was for her.

By the time I'd finished talking to Meg, Miss Henrietta had gone, and I had a job to catch up with her. I knew I would be in trouble, leaving her to wander alone like that, but I was so happy for my sister, and Miss Henrietta had been so kind to let me go and speak to her, I lost track of time.

I lied to Miss Cora and the Misses Molly and Dolly Marsh because I was afraid of being dismissed and sent away from Marsholm Manor.

The truth is that I didn't see the young man that Miss Henrietta says she met on that day.

3

Testimony of Henrietta Lakeham

It might be difficult for anyone to believe, after the dreadful crime I committed, but I went into my marriage determined to be a faithful and dutiful wife. I made Sir George wait three years before accepting his proposal. I wanted to be sure I was doing the right thing.

I suppose I also hoped that one day Max Parish would return. Or if not him, a suitor whom I felt I could love and who loved me. Remember I was eighteen years old when I met him — little more than a child really — and had a romantic nature. If not for Cora, who has more common sense, I might never have married. My cousin impressed upon me that Sir George's three years of devotion deserved some recognition.

'Dearest, you cannot keep the poor

man waiting any longer,' she said to me late one night, as a storm raged outside. She had come to my room, knowing that the storm would disturb me. 'He is pining away for love of you.'

About that she was wrong. Sir George and I never lied to each other about our feelings. He married me because he needed money to invest in his estate. I married him because I felt I had no other choice. I also saw it as a way of being free. From what I could not say. All I knew was that I imagined life in my own home, with a husband, as being different to the one I lived with Cora and the twins.

We honeymooned in Europe, staying away from England for six months. No doubt Dr Fielding will be disappointed to learn that I will not be discussing the intimate details of my marriage.

In many ways, Sir George was attentive and affectionate. We travelled to Greece, Italy, Switzerland and Austria, staying for a month or more at each place. I blossomed as we visited art galleries and museums, and I found my husband to be very knowledgeable. At those times we found a felicity that was missing in other areas of our life.

'You've changed,' George said to me one morning over breakfast.

'In what way?'

'You are no longer the frightened little rabbit that you were in England.'

'I am enjoying myself,' I said, surprised to find it was true. 'I hated living at the lodge.' I shivered, for it seemed that even mentioning that dark, dreary place made the sun shine a little less brightly. 'I'm sure it was haunted. I would often hear scratching behind the walls, or someone walking through the attic. Cora would tell me I was being silly, and no doubt I was. Still, I am glad we do not have to live there.'

On our return we went straight to my husband's home, Lakeham Abbey. I must confess to a feeling of dismay when I first saw it. My new home was a Gothic pile with flying buttresses, arched windows and an ornate façade.

In many ways the atmosphere was darker than that of the hunting lodge. Perhaps because there was so much more of the abbey, meaning more dark corners and secret places. It was all corridors and dull, lofty rooms. Many of the tapestries were damp, and had black mould growing up them.

I decided that I must make the best of things. Being away from the lodge for six months had helped to clear away some of the shadows that chased my dreams, so I decided to embrace my new home with enthusiasm.

'You must tell me the history,' I said to my husband as he helped me down from the coach. 'If it pleases you, Sir George.'

'I shall be delighted.'

The servants were all waiting in line to meet me. My first impression of them was that they were not amenable to me. The second thing I noticed was that Nan was not amongst them.

'Is my maid waiting inside?' I asked the housekeeper, Mrs Potter.

'We have set aside young Mary to be your maid, Lady Henrietta,' she said, looking at me as if I had impugned her housekeeping skills.

'I am sure Mary will be a very good maid,' I said, 'but Nan was supposed to be joining me.'

I heard a hesitant voice from the steps. 'Hetty . . . '

'Cora?' It is hard to explain how I felt on seeing my cousin there. I was happy. Of course I was happy. But it also felt as if the sun had disappeared behind a cloud.

I noticed a woman standing next to Cora. She was an older woman, small and mousy-looking, dressed in the fashions of yesteryear. I wondered who she was, but it was Cora who had my attention.

'I came to explain about Nan, dearest,' said Cora. 'But not now. You must be tired. Come on in and take a glass of champagne. Oh, but first you must meet your mother-in-law. Henrietta, this is Lady Lakeham.'

'How do you do,' I said, holding out my hand. 'I'm so sorry you could not come to my wedding, Lady Lakeham.'

'I was ill,' she said, looking around, as if for confirmation. Close up she seemed younger, and I guessed she could not have been very old when she married Sir George's father.

'Yes, George told me. I hope you are well now.'

'This abbey doesn't help, with its damp walls.'

'Yes, well, Mother,' said George, 'we don't really need to know about that, do we? It is good to see you again, Cora. Will you be staying long?'

'That is up to you and Hetty,' said Cora. 'You see . . . Oh, Hetty, I didn't want to tell you until you'd rested, but that ungrateful wretch Nan gave her notice several months ago. So I thought I would come and help until you found someone that you liked.'

'You cannot be my maid,' I said, horrified.

'Oh I am sure I should take to it

quite well,' said Cora. 'I can sew quite well, and I do need to earn a living. Molly and Dolly, though darlings and happy to help me, struggle on their income.'

'Then you shall be Lady Henrietta's companion,' said Sir George. 'What says you, Henrietta?'

'Oh, yes,' I said, perplexed by the way everything seemed to have been decided for me. 'Yes, that would be wonderful.'

It was much later before I was able to ask what had happened with Nan. Cora had insisted on coming to help me undress, telling Mary to go and help Lady Lakeham instead. It was just like my cousin to organise people. She did it so well.

'Dearest,' she said, hesitating as she began to brush my hair, 'I do not want to tell you. Just forget the silly girl.'

'Please, Cora. I want to know.'

'Well, you know that I think you are the sweetest creature who ever lived. It's just that no one else knows you like I do. Nan misunderstood your moods and assumed you were unhappy with her. So she said she would rather leave.'

'I thought she was my friend,' I whispered. Of everyone I had left behind to go on my honeymoon, Nan was the one I had most looked forward to seeing again.

'She was a servant, darling. Servants are never your friends.' Cora put her arms around my shoulders and smiled into the mirror. I always felt so plain when she was there, but I did not resent her beauty. 'I am your friend and I always have been, and now we are going to be closer than ever.'

As I got into bed that night, I shivered. The room I had been given did not help. It had high, dark ceilings, and the night breeze penetrated the walls and the ill-fitted windows. Every sound seemed to echo. I even thought I heard footsteps overhead, but told myself it must just be the servants going to bed, even when the sounds lasted well into the night when the rest of the household should have been asleep.

It occurred to me that I did not have to be alone. I could go to my husband. No one would question that. But the truth is — and I am sorry to disappoint Dr Fielding — my husband had no interest in my company. At least not in that way. It was something he had made plain from the first night of our marriage.

There I was, twenty-two years old, with a husband who did not find me desirable, a maid who had apparently hidden her distaste for me for years, and living in a house that already terrified me. If it is true and I am mad, is it any wonder?

In the past I might have sent for Nan. She had soothed me through many a nervous night. Instead I remembered a night, nearly four years earlier, when there were fairy lights in the trees and a handsome man came strolling through the dark. I might even have smiled as I fell asleep.

The wedding was very Elegant and it Should have been the Happiest day of Hetty's life. Instead she looked like a wet Dish rag, with her Face all Pale and Wan.

It was Unfortunate that Sir George's Mother did not attend. In fact, not many from His side did come to the Wedding. And our side are much Depleted, so that apart from a few servants and Friends from the County, it was just Us and Cora. Cora made Such an exquisite Maid of Honour, it was not Surprising that Hetty looked rather Dull by comparison.

Our lives at the Lodge settled down whilst Hetty was on her Honeymoon. The Tension that usually accompanied Hetty's presence went with her and for that We were Grateful. We can Assure you that we did not hear any Ghosts wandering the Halls at night. Not so much as a Creaky Floorboard.

Poor Cora was Unhappy, and we Did

our best to Cheer her, but she missed her cousin so much and she could Not wait till Hetty returned. Sometimes she would pace the room, saying, 'I wonder what they are doing now.' Or, 'I wonder where he is taking her today.' She would work Herself into such a Fever that it was all we could do to Calm her down.

'Even when Hetty is not here, you let her cause you distress, dear,' we said.

Cora laughed and said, 'You are right. But I have been taking care of her for so long, dear aunts. I hate to think of her being away from me.'

We were There on the Day that Nan left our employment. We do not remember exactly when it Happened, but are sure that dear Cora was correct when she said it was Several months before Hetty returned from her Honeymoon.

We heard such a Commotion early in the morning, just as We were Dressing. Nan was Shouting, 'I won't go! I don't want to go. I am sick of the mood swings and always feeling as if I am walking on eggshells. I'd leave if I didn't think it would do more harm than good.'

Cora told her to Leave if she felt that way. Nan refused, saying that Cora did not pay her Salary. Really, to talk of Money in such a Vulgar way.

Cora came running upstairs to us Whispering, 'Poor Hetty. What can I do, dear aunts? You know how she is, and how things affect her. I cannot ever tell her what Nan has said, and yet we cannot let that girl remain here knowing she is so hostile to our darling.'

For the Avoidance of any Doubt, we were the ones who told Nan to leave. We went downstairs and told her to Get Out of the house Immediately.

'You're making a big mistake,' Nan said. 'You indulge her too much. You always have. She's dangerous! One of these days something awful will happen and it will all be your fault, you stupid, gullible old women!'

Well, such Insolence was Unsupportable. We told Nan that if she did not

Leave quietly, we would Give her a bad Reference. She left soon after that and Good Riddance to her, we say.

Poor Cora was Stricken. 'How can I explain this to Hetty?'

'You must tell her the Truth,' we replied. 'It is time we stopped Pussy-footing around the girl. Nan was Right about one thing: We all walk on Eggshells when Hetty is here.'

As much as it Pains us, we are also forced to admit that Nan was correct about something awful Happening. It is true that something Unspeakable may have already Happened, though the details are, and Always have been, rather Foggy.

But how could we Possibly have known the Horror that would go with Hetty to Lakeham Abbey?

Testimony of Henrietta Lakeham

Over the months that followed, we began to settle into a routine at

Lakeham Abbey. Cora and I would spend the morning in my sitting room, reading or doing needlepoint. Sir George went riding or taking part in those other pursuits that country men find so irresistible. I would have liked to go riding, but there was only one good horse in the stables; and whilst I might have gone in the afternoon, it did not seem fair to work the poor horse so hard. In the afternoon Sir George would go and visit the estates, whilst Cora and I walked out or, if the weather was not amenable, sketched or continued with our needlepoint.

We ate luncheon with Sir George and his mother. It was always a strained affair. Lady Lakeham did not offer much in the way of conversation. Sometimes only Cora and I would speak, but as we had already spent the morning together, our discussions often faltered. My husband was only slightly less reticent than his mother, until one got him onto the subject of Lakeham Abbey.

'It fell into the Lakeham family's hands after the dissolution of the monasteries,' he explained one day at luncheon. He had promised to tell me about the house when we first returned, but he had much to do on the estate so there had been little time. Desperate for some conversation — I must admit to missing Aunts Molly and Dolly; they may have clucked like a couple of old hens, but at least mealtimes were never silent — I asked him to tell me more.

I thought it might endear me to him somewhat if I showed interest in his home. At this time I was still determined to be the dutiful wife.

'Yes,' he continued after taking a drink of wine, 'one of my ancestors did a good turn for Henry VIII, and the abbey was his reward, along with a baronetcy. Unfortunately, little money went with it, which is where I hope you will help me, Henrietta.'

'Of course,' I agreed. 'The house is in need of modernisation.'

'The house is perfect as it is,' said

Lady Lakeham. I was surprised to hear her speak up.

'Yes, of course, it's wonderful. But it might benefit from more light and . . . ' I faltered under her hostile gaze. 'I did not mean to insult your house, Lady Lakeham.'

'But it is your house now,' Cora said. 'Is that not right, Sir George?' She looked at my husband archly. I knew she was only protecting my interests, but I wished she had not said anything. I did not want to make an enemy of Lady Lakeham. 'If Henrietta is to put money into the house, then I think she should have some say in how it is spent.'

'It is a wife's duty to obey her husband,' said Lady Lakeham.

The air crackled with tension. That old feeling of apprehension, which I thought I had lost, came flooding back.

'Please, tell me more about the house, Sir George,' I said, trying to bring calm to troubled waters.

'What Hetty wants are the ghost

stories,' said Cora, laughing and rolling her eyes.

'No,' I said, 'I do not.'

'Yes you do. You were always asking Molly and Dolly to tell you them, even though it scared you.'

I opened my mouth to protest but nothing came out.

'Then ghost stories she shall have,' said Sir George.

'I would rather know about the living people who inhabited the house,' I said, my voice sounding weak, even to myself.

'We will all meet in the library after dinner tonight,' he said, ignoring me. 'Then I shall tell you all about the spirits that walk in the abbey.'

I think I excused myself then, feeling sick and dizzy. Even on my honeymoon, with a man who did not want me, I had not felt so nervous. The years slipped away and I was a frightened child again. The walls of Lakeham Abbey began to close in on me, and I saw mockery and hatred in the face of every gargoyle or every ancestor who decorated the corridor walls. All told me that I did not belong there, and I longed for Marsholm Manor, the home of my childhood. Despite the darkness that had accompanied me for so long, I felt safe then.

I do not remember where that fear began. I suppose it must have been when I lost my parents. Given the circumstances, it is not surprising. It is the one thing I have been unable to discuss, despite Dr Fielding's coaxing and threat of cold baths. I did not need the ghosts that my husband or Aunts Molly and Dolly cooked up. I had enough ghosts and apparitions of my own to contend with.

The truth is that when I was ten years old, my parents died in a brutal manner. As if that were not bad enough, I was the one who found them, and the image of them lying in a pool of blood haunts me still.

4

From the notes of Dr Fielding

So now we come to the truth of the patient's past. Or at least she touches upon it. I have had to learn what really happened from Miss Cora.

The dear young lady was reluctant to tell me. 'There is no proof,' she whispered hoarsely. 'And I have told myself that Hetty could not have done such a thing. She was only ten years old.'

'Children have killed before, and they will again,' I told her. 'Please, dear Miss Cora, tell me. For I can see this is a burden you have been carrying for a long time.'

'It was over something so trivial,' she said, closing her eyes as if to hide the pain within them. 'A dress that did not fit quite well enough, or a bonnet with the wrong colour ribbons. It was something of the sort. Such things always distressed poor Hetty, and she was inconsolable. I think she knew that she would never be a great beauty, and this disturbed her mind, so that everything she wore had to be perfect. Well she railed and railed against this garment until she was inconsolable. My aunt and uncle had no choice but to send her to bed without any supper. I remember my Uncle Julius saying, 'We have made too many allowances for her, Charlotte. It is time we were stricter.''

Miss Cora wiped her eyes with a delicate lace handkerchief. 'I wanted to go with Hetty, as I was sure I could reason with her, but they refused. 'She must learn her lesson,' Uncle Julius said, 'even if it means her being alone. Only then will she realise that if she does not alter her ways, she could end up alone for the rest of her life.' Oh, he was angry that night. I had never seen him so out of sorts. I went to my own room and cried and cried.

'It was later — much later — that I heard someone walking along the corridor. I opened my door and saw Hetty walking towards Uncle Julius and Aunt Charlotte's room. They were rather out of fashion in that they shared a bedroom. I always thought it very romantic, but it was to be their undoing. If they had not insisted on staying together, one of them might have survived. I did not know that at the time that anything would happen. You must realise, I was but sixteen years old, and ignorant of the horrors that stalk this world.'

'Of course, dear lady. How could you have known? No one will blame you,' I said. I wanted to put my arms around her, but that would have been inappropriate.

'It is rare to find such kindness in this world,' she said. I was more than happy to be her saviour.

'Tell me, dear lady, what happened next?'

'I went back into my room at first, thinking that perhaps my cousin had gone to apologise, as she had so many times before. Then I heard an unholy ruckus coming from my aunt and uncle's chamber. At first I was too afraid to leave my room . . . ' She lapsed into silence, and I understood that she was struggling to tell me about the horror.

'Where were your aunts — erm, Molly and Dolly? Surely they heard something. As adults they should have dealt with this. Not you, a mere child at the time.' She looked little more than a child now, with her big blue eyes and smooth forehead. She was so gentle, so trusting. Perhaps too trusting.

'We were in the west wing, and they had their own suite of rooms all the way over in the east wing. But it was lucky that we both were unable to sleep that night, and heard the commotion. Only by the time they got to us, it was too late.'

'I see. Go on, dear lady.'

'Things went silent, and I told myself that I had imagined the commotion. I wanted to go to sleep, but I could not. So I went into the corridor, and I saw that the door to my aunt and uncle's room was open. I went in, terrified of what I might find, and saw Hetty lying on the floor, surrounded by their . . . their bodies.' She gulped back a sob. 'It must have been some itinerant breaking in. That often happened in Marsholm Cell. Only the week before, Uncle Julius had dealt with a man on the bench — Uncle was a magistrate — and he feared he had been too soft in letting the man go on his way. What if that man had come and taken his revenge?'

'For being set free?' I asked.

'No, you are correct, Dr Fielding. It does not make sense. But how can I believe that dear Hetty would do such a thing? And yet, now . . . '

'Miss Cora, if you believe your cousin is guilty of something, you must hand her over to the police.'

She shook her head vehemently. 'I will not. I cannot. She does not know what she is doing when this, this . . . '

'Madness?'

'Yes, when this madness overtakes her. I truly believe she goes into some sort of fugue state. Please, keep her here where she is safe and cannot be a danger to others. I am willing to keep paying you the extra funds to do so. Or will you betray me and go the police?'

'I will not betray you, dear lady,' I promised. Her devotion to her cousin moved me, even if I did not believe that Lady Henrietta deserved such loyalty.

I have had a chance to observe Her Ladyship for several weeks, and I am convinced that despite her occasional moments of anguish, she is not mentally incapable of understanding right from wrong. In fact, I would go so far as to say she is saner than anyone else at the hospital, including me.

This begs the question of whether she *is* insane . . . or just evil.

63

Testimony of Constable Jacob Richards
(retired)

I was the constable in Marsholm Cells at the time that Mr and Mrs Marsh were brutally murdered. It was a sorry affair, leaving a young lady orphaned, with only her cousin and two rather ridiculous aunts for company. There was one young woman, called Nan, who worked as a maid, and who seemed to have quite a bit of common sense.

But Nan said that on that night she had slept soundly. In fact, she slept so well that she did not wake up until late the following morning, by which time everything was done and dusted. This earned her a reprimand from the Misses Molly and Dolly Marsh.

Mr and Mrs Marsh were found in their room, and both had been attacked rather brutally with a knife. We never did find the knife in question, and can only assume that the murderer — whom we believed to be a passing tramp — had taken it with him.

I admit that there were some elements that disturbed me. At the time I was walking out with the laundress, Mrs Harris — now my good wife — and she said that some nightdresses were missing from the laundry order. It seemed that all the ladies in the house had three nightdresses each. Laundry is not of much interest to me, even though my dear wife is, so I was rather confused about her going on about there usually being 'three nightgowns each — one to wear, one in the drawer, and one in the laundry. But that's not the same anymore.' I did not really listen.

I am ashamed to say that it was not the nightgowns of the young ladies at Marsholm Manor that interested me at the time. Not that I was interested in anyone's nightgown, you understand. Suffice to say, I was a man in love and had other things on my mind.

Enquiries at the house yielded nothing, with Molly and Dolly Marsh becoming increasingly confused. They would not be budged from that point. Nor would they back down about where they were when the murder took place, even though I did an experiment with my assistant, Sykes.

I must admit it never once occurred to me that Miss Henrietta Marsh was capable of such a crime. She was but ten years old at the time and the sweetest child imaginable. I had heard — I forget who told me — she was spoiled and wilful, with a violent streak, but I only ever remember her behaving in a gracious and ladylike manner.

It is hard to explain what a person goes through when dealing with local nobility. You're always on the back foot, because it does not do to anger them. I relied on the good will of the local landowners to keep my job as the constable. Any wrong step would have resulted in me losing that job. As I was fifty years old at the time, I had little hope of finding other employment.

In light of what has happened since, I realise that I have been very remiss in my duties. As I look back, I feel ashamed of myself. Had I pushed harder for answers to my questions, the ensuing tragedies might have been avoided.

Testimony of Henrietta Lakeham

The darkness has haunted me for as long as I can remember. Sometimes, for no apparent reason, I would feel as if I wanted to scream at some unknown terror.

It was not as bad when my parents were alive and we lived at Marsholm Manor. Despite the ghosts that were supposed to walk its dark hallways, Mother and Father always brought light and laughter to my life.

I fear I was not always the child they wished me to be. Sometimes I would catch them looking at me pensively, and Cora would say to me, 'What have you done now, Hetty?' I could never quite remember, but assumed there must have been something wrong with my behaviour.

I remember little of the night they died, when I was ten years old; only that it had been a dreadful, distressing day full of tears and anger. I know I cried myself to sleep because of something I had wanted to do but was not allowed to. I was woken by my mother calling me, though Cora told me that was not possible, because she had been dead some time when they were found. I went to their room and after that, I recall nothing — except the red mist, which seemed to run from the carpet all the way up the walls.

Cora found me unconscious and carried me to my room, where she changed my nightgown and threw it on the fire. I drifted in and out of consciousness, but I remember that it, too, appeared to be covered in the red mist. 'At least no one will find that,' she said, though I did not understand why it mattered.

I remember being asked questions I

could not answer, and Cora at my side the whole time, holding my hand tight and refusing to let me be alone with anyone. 'They might make you say something you regret,' she whispered to me when the magistrate — the one who replaced Father — was on his way one day.

The story was that an itinerant had broken into the house and murdered my parents, but that was not possible. The doors were always locked at night, and as far as I know, there were no secret passageways in the manor.

After that, both Cora and Aunts Molly and Dolly treated me almost as if I were an invalid. Particularly when we moved to the hunting lodge, so that Marsholm Manor might be ready for our distant cousin.

The darkness that had only occasionally crept in when I was a child began to descend more often. I became afraid of my own shadow. Afraid of saying and doing the wrong thing, for reasons I could not explain. It always felt that when things went wrong, it was my fault, because I had forgotten to say or do something I should have said or done.

It sometimes seemed to me that life was an ordeal to be got over with very quickly. Only the memory of Mama and Papa's smiles stopped it from encroaching too much. That and dear, sensible Nan, who came with us and always did her best to care for me. At least until I drove her away.

I wonder if that is what I am fated to do all my life — drive away those who love me. Only Cora remains loyal, but how much longer can she defend the indefensible? If I am a killer, then I deserve to be punished for my crimes. If only I could remember what had happened.

I must think of happier things, for to look forlorn for one minute invariably leads to one of Dr Fielding's treatments. I do not worry too much about them, however. I have found that if I'm docile and do as I am told, it is all over

70

with very quickly. Those who struggle suffer the most. So I behave, and then I am allowed back to my room, which is most peaceful; and it is also where I have a view of the park.

There is a lake in the distance that reminds me of the one at Lakeham Abbey. Strange as it may seem, I was very happy on the island in the middle of that lake. For it was there that I saw him again.

Living at Lakeham Abbey, I was once more forced to watch what I said. Invariably any comment by me would lead to my husband or his mother's disapproval. Dear Cora would jump in to defend me, and then there would be a huge argument. She tried so hard to make my husband care for me, to no avail.

'Do you not think Hetty looks very pretty today?' she would ask him at luncheon.

'What? Yes, I suppose so.'

'Then for goodness sake, man, tell her.'

'Cora . . . ' I protested.

'No, I cannot sit silent. I see how unhappy you are, darling and I believe Sir George should bless his luck in finding such a lovely wife. You may not be on a par with the fashionable ladies he knows in London, but you are more than a match for any lady for the county.'

I wondered about the ladies in London, where Sir George often visited. Was there a particular woman there? I wanted to ask, but the argument that ensued got in the way.

So I took to walking in the grounds after luncheon as often as I could. I reasoned that if I were not there, my husband could not snub me, and Cora could not get angry about it. I also hoped that the exercise would make me sleep so heavily that I did not hear the strange sounds at night, which broke my slumber on a regular basis.

I had been married for a couple of years when he returned to me. I was on one of my regular walks, avoiding an argument about Sir George asking me for more money to improve the estate. Cora went on the defensive immediately. 'Do you wish her to spend every penny on you so that there is nothing left for your children?'

I had not admitted to my cousin that there would be no children. I let her believe that my marriage was normal in that respect. But I did not want to get into another long discussion about funds. I had already given Sir George twenty thousand pounds, and yet had seen very little change to the estate. He explained that the builders he had employed found better-paying employment elsewhere, but would return in the winter. Winter had come and gone, and they still did not return.

Did I believe this? I am not as foolish as some might think. I have already said that I know my husband had married me for my money. His mother was often dressed in old clothes. The carpets were frayed, and the curtains threadbare. Yet I could see very little of the funds I provided going on the estate.

Apart from to the servants. When I found out how poorly they were paid, I made it my business to improve their wages. I will not go into the argument that caused! Even Cora was upset with me about that and did not speak to me for three days. She said that I should not buy peoples' love and affection. She was right, of course, but I had no thoughts of that. At least I do not think so.

On that day, I had gone out to avoid another upsetting scene. The day was bright and cheerful, and even the abbey looked better in the sunshine.

Below the plantation lay a lake of surpassing beauty. I liked to sit there and sketch. As the marshy ground was often wet and muddy, Cora refused to go there. After a while I had become bolder, and began taking a small rowing boat out to the island in the centre of the lake. From there I could see the house, but I was fairly certain that no one could see me.

It had become my place. Somewhere there were no arguments, no creaky stairs and no strange banging sounds. Sometimes I would take a nap, and then return to the abbey refreshed and almost in the right frame of mind to face the next onslaught.

On that day, after rowing across to the island, I stepped out onto the grassy bank; and because it had been raining in the night, I almost lost my footing. Strong arms caught me, and at first I was alarmed. Had my husband found my hiding place? I looked up to find dark blue eyes gazing back at me.

'Hello, Henrietta,' Max said.

I had heard that young ladies sometimes swooned in the presence of handsome men, but considered it a foolish sort of thing for a girl to do. On that day I was nearly as foolish, and only just managed to avoid making a complete fool of myself.

In my defence, I think it was relief that I finally had a friend of my own at

Lakeham Abbey. Yes, of course I had Cora, but she was too close to me to be of much help. Max represented someone who was not emotionally involved in the darkness in my life. He was the light that illuminated all the dull corners.

'You're here,' I said, somewhat redundantly.

'Yes, I'm here. How are you?' He took my arm and led me away from the bank. I suspected he was making sure we were out of sight of the house, but I did not mind. He was there, standing beside me, tall and handsome.

'I am well. I am . . . ' To my eternal shame I burst into tears. He let me cry for a long time, simply holding me close against his chest.

'It is all right, my love,' he said. 'I am here now.'

'I don't know what's wrong with me,' I said, pulling away. 'You must think me a silly woman.'

'No, I don't think that at all, Hetty, and that's something you must always remember.'

I wondered at him using the diminutive of my name, but did not question him because it seemed right. 'Where have you been?' I asked. 'I waited . . . I mean, I wondered what happened to you when you went to the colonies.'

'I was in the West Indies,' he said. 'Much has changed since I last saw you. Then I was a poor man, but now I am not.'

'I do not care,' I said. 'I never did. You must believe that.'

'But *I* cared,' he insisted. 'I am not the sort of man who would happily live off my wife's money.' He glanced towards the abbey and I knew of whom he was thinking.

'How did you know?'

'I have asked questions round and about. I wanted to be sure he was being kind to you.'

'He is a very attentive husband,' I said. Or at least he had been. 'He does not treat me cruelly, if that's what you mean.'

'Good, because I've never killed a man, but I might have to make an exception in his case if I thought he had harmed you in any way.'

You cannot imagine what it does to a woman's heart to hear a man talk of her in such a way; especially a woman who has not been loved by anyone since she was a little girl.

'How did you come here?' I asked. 'To this island?'

'We've been watching you for a while, to learn your movements and find out the best time for me to come.'

'We?'

'I cannot say any more, Hetty. But, know that you do have friends who care for you.'

'I have Cora.'

'Yes, of course, you have Cora,' he said, but he did not sound very convinced.

'She does her best to stick up for me.'

I could see him wrestling with something, but then he appeared to change his mind. 'Hetty,' he said, and I realised with a thrill that he was still holding me in his arms, 'there are people in that house whom you cannot trust. Not even amongst the servants, despite you being an absolute angel and paying them more.'

I stood back a little. 'You really do know a lot!'

'I've made it my business to. Things are . . . delicate, Hetty. Not least because of your reputation. I will do nothing to destroy that, unless there is no other choice. But we will get together again and plan your escape from this godforsaken place.'

'My escape?'

'Are you telling me that you want to stay with your husband? If that is the case, say the word and I will bother you no more. You owe me nothing. I want to make that clear. Even if we do get you out of here, I expect nothing that you do not willingly give to me. I act in these matters as your friend. Whatever happens later is a discussion for another time. You need rest and you need freedom. But only if you want it.'

I nodded. 'Yes. Yes, I want freedom. My husband does not love me and I do not love him.' I wanted to tell him more. I wanted him to know that if I went with him, it would be as his alone. Shyness prevented me.

'I have to go now,' he said reluctantly, looking at his pocket watch. 'I don't want to, but I must. Your cousin will come looking for you soon.'

'Yes, she usually does after about half an hour.' That had not been the case until the past couple of weeks, but Cora had been concerned about me.

'You can't tell her about me, Hetty. She will never let you leave.'

'Because of my reputation, you mean. No, you're right; Cora would worry too much about me being ruined. She might not understand that I do not care, as long as I am happy and with someone whom I . . . ' I faltered. I had seen him but three times, and there I was, almost pouring my heart out to him.

He did not reply immediately. 'It is best if I say no more. Let us keep this as our secret.'

I agreed, and was quite happy to do so. For the first time in my life, I had something of my own. Something I did not have to share with someone else. So I kept my meetings with Max a secret for as long as I could.

When I returned to the abbey that afternoon, everything seemed less bleak and cold. The sunshine helped, I suppose, but so did my mood.

Cora was waiting for me in my sitting room. 'Dearest, where have you been?' she said, running to embrace me. 'I've been worried.'

'Just walking,' I said. 'Down at the lake.'

'Darling, you know how dangerous those marshes are. Sir George has told us about his ancestor who sank into the mud and died of suffocation.' She paused. 'You look different.'

'The sun is shining and the world is a beautiful place.'

'I'm glad you think so,' she said, clearly upset. 'Because I am afraid I have to leave you, and I cannot bear it.'

'Why? What has happened?'

'Sir George says. I told him that if it were up to me, you would refuse to give him any more money.'

'Then I will give it to him,' I said. I did not care anymore. 'Whatever he asks for. I've already lost Nan. I won't let him drive you away.'

'Oh, dear heart, are you sure? I feel such a burden to you. I'm afraid I always have been.'

'No, of course not. You've been my best friend.'

'Been?' She looked perplexed by my use of the past tense.

'You *are* my best friend. Of course you are.'

I cannot deny that someone else had replaced her in my affections. All I could think about was Max. If there were strange sounds in the old abbey that night as I settled down to sleep, I neither heard nor cared.

Dr Fielding's Notes

Now that I know the man called Max does not exist, the patient's hysteria becomes clearer. She is married to a man who, due to not being physically attracted to her, has not consummated their marriage. So once again she turns to her imaginary friend.

The dream man represents her escape from a loveless marriage. The fact they meet — in her fantasies at least — on the island represents some far-off shore, where they will spend their lives happily with no thoughts of the more mundane aspects of life. What I want to understand is how the patient became so enamoured of the fantasy world she created that she came to the conclusion her husband must die.

I had hoped to ask Miss Cora, but sadly she has not visited for several weeks. She sent me a very pretty note explaining her absence. She is abroad 'to try to forget', she said. She promises she will return — and sort out the matter of the overdue bill — very soon.

I want to give the young lady time to pay, of course; but if she cannot, then I fear that the patient will have to be moved to one of the free establishments for the insane. As these are little better than prisons, I am sure Miss Cora will not leave her cousin to such a fate.

5

Testimony of Molly and Dolly Marsh

It was so Thrilling to be invited to Lakeham Abbey. We had not often left Marsholm Cells, and when Cora and Hetty left us, our neighbours were not as Quick with their Invitations. We understand how Difficult it is, when one invites Unmarried ladies, to find enough Men to partner them. But a Supper invitation once or twice in the Week would have been Pleasant, and saved us considerable Expenditure on our housekeeping.

Unless one is a Spinster, one cannot understand the Penury that we Suffer. As it is, we can Only afford one cook, one butler — who doubles as a footman when needed — and two maids. Poor dear Cora understands, for like us, she has been left at the Mercy of someone else's Charity.

We do not deny that Hetty was Generous with Cora, just as she was with us when she lived at the lodge; but after her Marriage, she Hardly sent us any Money. We Thought we had been forgotten.

'It was Hetty's idea,' she told us when we arrived at that Elegant abode. We have no Doubt that it was Cora's idea, but we greeted Hetty with the Affection as we have Always shown her.

What a wonderful home Sir George owned. True, it was in need of Modernisation. Even our lodge had indoor Ablutions. But the Nobility do not have to Worry about having the Best of everything. Their Breeding speaks for itself. This we found in the Dowager Lady Lakeham. She embodied *noblesse oblige* in every pore, and even Deigned to speak to us from time to time.

At luncheon one day, she asked one of us to 'Pass the gravy, please'. Sadly, in our Scramble to please her, and unsure which one of us she Addressed, we ended up spilling it all over the table. But she was so Gracious about it, even though, as she said to Sir George, 'Any more of this and the tablecloth will be unusable.' She may have been Referring to the day before, when one of us — we forget which — was so nervous that we Dropped a glass of red wine.

Of course, Hetty did not make things Much better by trying to Stick up for us and becoming rather upset. Had she not spoken up, we are Sure the dowager would have forgotten it. But that was Hetty — Always stumbling in where Angels feared to Tread.

'Aunts,' Cora said, when she came to kiss us Goodnight, 'do you not think that Hetty has got worse?'

We agreed that Indeed she had. The girl was as Skittish as a Kitten.

'She is again claiming she can hear voices at night, and people walking above her bedroom. But this is impossible. Those rooms are not occupied. I am afraid,' Cora said, taking Both our hands.

'I am so afraid that she will do something awful . . . again.'

She did not Have to tell us what she Meant. We had been there when our Brother and his wife were Brutally Slain. We saw Hetty lying at their Side with our Very own Eyes. Not that the constable Believed us. He even Contradicted us and said we could Not have, because we were in the Other wing. But we Know what We saw.

Then there was that Strange thing about the Nightgowns with which Constable Richards intruded. To think of a Man discussing a lady's Private garments in such a way. 'There is nothing wrong with the nightgowns in this house,' we told him. 'They are of the most modest design.' Then he went on about how Some nightgowns were Missing. Well, what Business was that of His? We Told him as Much.

After that, he started to Question where we had been and What had brought us from the east wing to the west wing. Well, of course the Tragedy did. Then he did a very Strange thing and asked us to Wait for him in Our rooms, whilst he Looked around the west wing with his young Assistant.

Later the constable Knocked on our sitting room Door and asked if we had heard Anything all morning. 'No, we have not,' we said, not even Sure why he was Asking.

He spoke in the most Insolent manner, saying, 'I thought not. Which is a pity, as I've just murdered young . . . ' oh, whatever his Name was. 'And very noisily too.'

He could not have Murdered young what's his name, because we saw them Walking away from the house together, Laughing.

Then we Had to go and live in the Hunting Lodge, because Marsholm Manor had to be vacated for the distant cousin who had inherited. That he could not give a Home to the Sisters and Child of the one who had given him the Benefit of a manor house and acres of Ground is something we will never Understand.

We have dealt with the Hunting Lodge, have we not? Yes, we Believe so. We were discussing our trip to Lakeham Abbey and the Gracious Dowager Lady Lakeham. What that Poor woman must have endured . . .

We are getting ahead of ourselves. We have so Much to tell about the events leading up to the Tragedy.

As usual, when Hetty was present, the Atmosphere was Strained and Unhappy. Yet she looked very Content, compared to her usual Nervous manner. Particularly in the Afternoon after she had been for a Walk. Of course we know why now. The poor, Deluded creature.

It was Cora who Asked for our help in that Matter. One evening, after dinner, when we met in the Drawing room (how refined!), we had been sharing stories of the Ghosts of Marsholm Manor. Sir George, by turns, told stories of Lakeham Abbey. There was one Particular story about a young man and his brother.

'He was always jealous of his younger

brother,' Sir George told us, by the Flickering light of the fire. It was rather a Sorry affair, and we Considered asking for more coal, but felt it would be Impertinent. It had been raining for nearly a week, which did nothing for our poor old bones in such a Draughty house. Not that we Complained. To be in such a place, with Nobility, was a Dream come true for us.

'So one day, after a period of heavy rain,' Sir George continued, 'he took his brother for a walk in the marshes. The younger child went into the mud and never came out. Of course everyone said it was an accident, but the elder brother later bragged to a school friend of seeing off his sibling. They say that on some days of the year, especially when it has been raining, one can hear the younger brother crying for help as the mud swallows him up.'

We screamed in Horror, imagining that Tragic child. It was just too Awful. 'Tell us more,' we cried. 'Tell us more.'

Hetty had been in one of her Moods

for a few days. Cora said it was because she could not go out for her Daily walk, due to the Precipitation. As we asked for More stories, she Stood up and said, 'I think I will retire. I am tired of such tragedies being presented as entertainment. It is not entertaining to talk of murder and loss. If the story is true, a mother and father no doubt grieved for the child, just as a child will grieve for her parents when they die.'

'Hetty, dearest,' said Cora, looking at Sir George with Anger in her eyes. We could see that they did not Like each other very Much, even though Sir George had Treated us with Great kindness. 'I have told them not to upset you so, but they don't listen.' Hetty merely Glared at her. Poor Cora, trying so Hard to help, and Hetty repaid her with anger.

At that, Sir George got up and Stormed from the room, saying something like, 'I cannot do this anymore.'

Of course he Meant that he did not intend to continue his marriage to

Hetty. And that is probably why she Believed he had to Die.

The next day, the weather was Warmer, but the ground still Wet. When Hetty had gone for her walk, Cora came to us and said, 'Dear Aunts, please follow her and make sure she is safe. She is becoming more and more unhinged. I do fear that one day she will do something reckless.'

We saw it as our Christian duty to keep an eye on Hetty. Cora had told us that Julius and Charlotte had talked of Sending her away when she was a child. Would that they had. Then this awful Thing would never have happened.

We followed her, at a Distance, as far as the Marshland near to the lake. We dared go no further, for fear of being Swallowed up by the Mud. Hetty seemed to care Nothing for that, even as the hem of her gown became Damp and Muddied. She climbed into a Small rowing boat, and rowed out to the Island in the centre.

We discussed whether We might find

a Boat and follow her, but we Feared being Drowned in the lake if we even Attempted such a thing. We were able to get a little closer, Sticking to the Dry land, but risking our Lives in the process. We could hear her Talking, and it seemed that someone was answering her in a Deep voice. We Wondered who that might be, but it was Cora who put us Straight.

We might have Stayed until she Rowed back, but one of us slipped in the mud, with the Other following soon after as we Scrambled for purchase. Our Screaming no doubt Alerted Hetty to our presence, because she was soon Rowing back.

Her face was Flushed and her eyes red, as if she had been crying. Yet she looked strangely at peace and Uncharacteristically beautiful. We have often Wondered if this was when she decided on her Course of Action.

When we told Cora later, she said, 'It is worse than I thought. She not only imagines this man, but she plays his part too. Would you not say, dear aunts, the deeper voice sounded very much like Hetty's?' We had to Concede that much was True.

Hetty helped us back to the house, which we Admit was Kind of her. We had to Change our Clothing, which was in a Dreadful state. We hoped the Servants would take care of it, as we owned very Few dresses, but we were to be Disappointed. We supposed that the Events of that night Prevented the house from being run Correctly, though our Mother always said that a Good servant will Continue his duties even when a Family is stricken by Tragedy.

The sad fact is that our Gowns have Never been returned to us, which for two women of Limited means is rather Unfortunate.

Of course, not as Unfortunate as what Did happen.

It was that Night when Cora took Hetty away, Impressing on us how we Must protect her from Investigation by the police. Cora also Insisted we leave the House that very night, and travel home so that we would not be Drawn into any scandal. We do not know how she Prevented the police from becoming involved, but she has always been a clever girl.

We Must say that we have been Vilified beyond belief for our actions, and this has Caused us great distress. His Grace has been Particularly scathing. But as Cora said, we Could not have the name of the Marshes Blackened any further.

We Maintain, as we have always Maintained, that we saw the scene ourselves, with our Very Own Eyes. There was a commotion during the night. Someone screamed, and we ran into the corridor, finding poor dear Cora in a Faint in the corridor on the Upper floor.

Hetty stood there with a Knife in her hand, Repeating over and over 'I have killed him. I have killed him.'

6

Testimony of Henrietta Lakeham

I remember Cora saying how wonderful it would be if we could have the aunts coming to visit. 'It will brighten up this dull house,' she said.

I must admit to some misgivings. My aunts, though loquacious, were not known for being particularly cheerful. On the other hand, at least they did talk, which was more than could be said for my husband and his mother.

My main concern was more selfish. I feared that if they were there, I would not be able to go and see Max on the island. Whilst we could not meet every day, our irregular rendezvous were the only thing that kept me sane during those dark times at Lakeham Abbey.

It was not only for the love of him — and I had come to love him dearly. It was the knowledge that I had a friend who did not judge me if I were feeling forlorn. He listened as I told him about my life, and he had a way of asking the right questions, even if the answers were somewhat painful to me.

I began to realise that no one had ever truly listened to me. Oh, Cora and Aunts Molly and Dolly would do their best to soothe my fears, but they also brushed them away as if they were inconsequential. I daresay they found me tiresome.

I think Nan would have listened, but her status in the house prevented our being friends on an equal footing, and sometimes I think Cora was jealous of her. My cousin often seemed to resent me spending time with my maid. I can understand that. Cora had no one else. Even though she was prettier than I, and more outgoing, she was only invited to local functions if I were, and I was invited rarely because people did not like me. So Cora preferred to keep me to herself, which made me feel guilty if I spent too much time with Nan. I did regret not hearing more of my maid's cheerful no-nonsense chatter, but I did not want to cause undue pain to my cousin.

It was about Cora that Max and I talked that day, and it was one of the rare times we exchanged harsh words. But first I want to explain about what happened before my aunts came to stay, as it might explain my state of mind and why he made me so angry.

Prior to my aunts' arrival, life at Lakeham Abbey had become increasingly strained. There had been several days of rain, meaning I could not go out. And at night I was afflicted with the same old fears as I heard sounds around the house. I even saw one of the ghosts.

It was late one night, and the wind howled outside. Up above me, as I lay in my bed alone, I heard footsteps. There were no servants on that corner of the house; their attic rooms were at the back of the abbey. The footsteps were closely followed by the sound of someone screaming and crying. I heard a thump, then the thunder of several pairs of feet.

No one else lived on that floor. My husband's rooms adjoined mine — the door remained locked on his side — and my cousin and the Dowager Lady Lakeham were along the hall. It seemed unlikely that they would go wandering at night.

The sudden noises were followed by a soft sobbing. As terrified as I was, I had to go and look. My candle was still lit — I did not like to sleep in the dark — so I got out of bed and took it with me.

It was freezing cold, for my husband would not allow coal to be used during the night, and I could see the breath coming from my lips as I walked the chilly corridor to the staircase at the end of the corridor. It was a part of the abbey I had never seen. In fact, despite living there for several months, there were many rooms I had not seen. No one had ever offered me a tour, and I had been too nervous to strike out alone in case I committed a faux pas.

Being with Max had given me a courage I had lacked in the past, and I was determined that I would lay this particular ghost to rest. There would be a reasonable explanation and I could stop feeling afraid. Besides, it was my home too; so, I told myself, I had the right to go where I pleased. In truth I had come to realise that Lakeham Abbey was not, and never would be, my home. I lied to myself about it being so to add courage to my endeavours.

Every stair seemed to creak as I climbed, and I felt sure I would be discovered. Again I told myself it did not matter. I was not intruding, because it was my home. I was Lady Lakeham.

First I found the room that would be above mine, only to find it full of dust and cobwebs. A big bed stood in the middle. As in my room, there were windows on two walls overlooking the grounds. I lowered my candle and saw a point in the wooden floor, near to the inner wall, where the dust had been disturbed, as if someone had been dragged on the floor. The trail stopped at the wall. I went over and put my hand on the wall.

I had heard that these old abbeys often had priest holes, though my husband had not mentioned such a thing at Lakeham. By this time I was excited at making a discovery and almost forgot my earlier fears. It was something of an adventure. I felt around the wall — the light from the candle showed that the wallpaper had a birds of paradise design — on which there was a grand mantelpiece, and pressed everything, hoping I might find a secret hideaway. All I found was dust and grime.

But something had happened in this room, I was sure of it. I went back out into the hallway, and was about to turn back to the stairs, when something — someone — grabbed my wrist. A scream died in my throat as I turned to find an old woman glaring at me. She was dressed in grey, and had matted silver hair.

'Leave,' she said. 'Leave this place.'

'I . . . who are you?'

'Just a ghost,' she said in rather plaintive tones. 'The ghost of Lakeham Abbey.'

She started to laugh, until her laughter turned to tears. I broke free and ran down the stairs, sobbing in terror.

Cora was waiting for me at the bottom of the stairs. 'Darling, what is it?' she said, catching me in her arms.

'An old woman . . . ' I managed to gasp. 'Upstairs.'

'Hetty, there is no one upstairs.'

'Yes there is. I saw her.'

'There is no one. Come along, dearest. Let me get you some water.'

I tried to convince her to follow me upstairs, but she was adamant she would not even look. She took me to my room and gave me a glass of water.

'Someone was up there,' I insisted.

'An old woman in grey.'

'That's just like in the story Sir George told us,' she said soothingly. 'Remember? When we first came to Lakeham?'

'No ... ' I remembered lots of stories, including one about a child drowning in the mud, but not that of a grey lady. I wanted to protest, but tiredness overwhelmed me and I fell asleep.

I developed a fever and kept to my bed for several days, overcome by great fatigue. Cora was at my side most of time, soothing me, giving me drinks of water and broth. My sleep was broken by lots of banging above, but whenever I tried to get up, exhaustion won and I went back to sleep again. I finally awoke late one morning, feeling more alert than I had for a while.

'I thought it best to leave you, dearest,' said Cora, bringing me a cup of tea. 'Now I want you to get dressed and come with me.'

When I had done as she asked, I

followed her into the hallway. My husband and mother-in-law were waiting for me. I hesitated, embarrassed, because they obviously knew what had happened.

'We just wish to alleviate your fears, Henrietta,' said Sir George. He looked irritated, as if I had put him to a lot of trouble.

Feeling even more nervous than I had the night before, I followed them up the stairs.

'Now,' said Cora, 'where did you find the room of which you spoke, dearest?'

I went to the area where the door should have been, but could not find it. 'I . . . it was here. There was a door here.'

'There is no door there now, Henrietta,' said Sir George. 'Is there?'

'But it was here! And this hallway was more derelict, and — '

'I have recently had it decorated,' said Sir George. 'But you saw it in the dark, did you not? Everything looks rather murky in the dark.'

I shook my head vehemently. I knew what I had seen, yet they were all looking at me as if I were mad.

'There must be something there,' I said. 'I am not an expert at architecture, but there must be a room in that space. I've seen the abbey from the outside and there are windows on this floor.'

'Of course there's a room, Henrietta,' said my husband. He spoke so mildly that I almost wanted to slap him. 'Come with me.'

He took a key from his pocket and led me to the next door along. Unlocking it, he led me in. 'It's an attic room,' he explained as I looked around, 'where we store all the old furniture and other things we have no further use for.'

Just as he had said, there was a room, twice the size of the one I had seen, packed full of furniture, trunks and old paintings. There was no wallpaper with birds of paradise, and no grand fireplace.

As I ran from the room into the corridor, I gasped when it seemed someone was running towards me. Then I realised that there was a mirror at the end of the corridor.

Notes of Dr Fielding

This latest extract from her journal shows how the patient is already beginning to have violent feelings towards her husband. She wishes to lash out at him because he does not believe her hysterical account, yet it is clear that he is showing her nothing but kindness and understanding.

The apparition is particularly interesting, and it is clear to me that the patient saw herself the night before. No doubt the words spoken by the 'ghost' were spoken by the patient, as she began to identify herself as an apparition to be feared.

I have received a letter from Miss Cora Marsh, who apologises for her absence. She warns me to keep watch on the patient, as she has enemies. I have had to write back and explain that the patient can no longer remain at St Jude's and that she will soon be moved to a public asylum.

Whilst I would welcome the chance to study the patient for longer, as she presents a most interesting case, her enemies are not my problem. I have been warned that my hospital is under investigation. It would seem I have my own enemies.

Testimony of Henrietta Lakeham

It started to rain soon after the incident with the ghost and the room that was not there. And it kept raining, even when my aunts arrived. I could not go and see Max on the island. Had I been able to, I know he would have helped me to talk through what happened and find a rational explanation to the events of that night.

I became more and more nervous. To make matters worse, I could see my husband and my cousin looking at me cautiously, as if they feared what else I might do. I could go nowhere and do nothing without them being close behind me, insisting on assisting me. I daresay they meant it kindly, but I began to feel suffocated. Even more so when my aunts arrived, and it became clear that they had been told all about my affliction. I hated being treated like an invalid. Even more, I hated it when my husband began to tell ghost stories. Whilst others listened with enjoyment, I felt I was being mocked for my fears.

When the sun shone for the first time in a week, nothing was going to keep me away from the island. I did not even know if Max would come, but I knew that just being there, where I had spent so many happy hours, would soothe my fevered brain.

He was there, and I ran into his arms. 'What is it?' he asked. 'What has happened? I've come every day, even in the rain. Where have you been?'

I somehow managed to blurt the whole story out, struggling to keep the tears back as I did so.

'They think I am mad. Do you think I am mad?' I asked.

'No, not at all. I think you have been sleep deprived, and tormented, but you are not mad.'

I relaxed against his chest. 'Thank you for that.'

He had me tell the story all over again, nodding as I described the second visit to the upper floor.

'And this was several days after you had gone to bed with a fever?' he said.

'Yes. I had such nightmares.'

'Of banging in the rooms above?'

'Yes.'

'Think, Hetty. You are an intelligent woman, despite the way your mind has been tormented. Think rationally. Why would there be banging on the floor above, after you had found the room?'

I turned away from him. What he was suggesting seemed unthinkable. But

110

had I not felt that way all my life?

'Tell me about Cora,' he said suddenly.

'My cousin?'

'Yes, your cousin, Cora.'

'She is my best friend. I have no one else here I can trust. Except for you.' I turned back to him. 'Take me away, Max. Please, take me away from this place. I have no money left, nothing I can offer you to help me, but — '

'I would not take your money,' he said, holding his head high. 'I do not care what you bring with you. But I cannot take you away yet. I will soon, I promise. There are investigations going on in the outside world that we hope will set you free. Do you remember the outside world, Hetty?'

'Hardly. We see no one here. I do not even know my neighbours. My husband . . . Sir George . . . does not care for society.'

'No, I'm sure he doesn't. As I said, there are things happening in the outside world, and steps are being taken to save you once and for all. But you must be patient. If you go with me now, it will ruin your reputation.'

'I do not care.'

'I do. I will not have you whispered about. You will leave Lakeham Abbey with your head held high, and with no blame on your part. I promise you that.'

'You do not want to help me,' I said, turning away again. 'Perhaps Cora is right. Perhaps you are a figment of my imagination. You are saying these things because even my imagination cannot bring about an escape from the situation in which I find myself.'

He took my shoulders and turned me back to face him. 'Can you feel my hands on your shoulders?'

'Yes.'

He moved closer. 'Can you feel my breath on your cheek?'

'Yes.'

'And can you feel this?' He lowered his head and his lips found mine. I had never been kissed until that moment. The sensation of his mouth on mine was so magical, so spiritual, that I was sure it must be a dream.

I shuddered against him as a sob rose in my throat. He held me in his arms until I was calmer. 'It feels real,' I whispered. 'I want it to be real.'

'It *is* real, as are my feelings for you.' He held me away from him. 'I need to talk to you about something.'

'About what?'

'Your cousin.'

'Cora?'

'Yes, Cora. I need to know how you feel about her, Hetty.'

'Well I am not in love with her,' I said, laughing. I blushed, realising what I had just admitted about my feelings for him.

'I should hope not. But what are your feelings about her?'

'I do not know.' I shrugged. 'She is my closest friend. I have no one else in my life, apart from you, whom I can trust.'

'Do you think she has your best interests at heart?'

'Of course she has. She always has. She seldom lets me out of her sight. She has always been there, making sure I behave.'

'Behave?'

'Because of my moods. Oh you do not know the half of it, Max. What a selfish and moody creature I can be.'

'How do you feel about Cora criticising you all the time?'

'She does not criticise. She just . . . ' I faltered, for now he had said it that way, I was not sure. 'I mean, she does not say that I have done wrong. She only wants me to be the best person I can be.'

'How does that make you feel?'

'I don't know. I am glad, I suppose that she steers me straight. I . . . ' I was about to say that I loved her, and that she was my dearest companion, but other feelings took over. 'I am sometimes annoyed with her,' I admitted. 'I wish she would not treat me as an invalid, especially as my husband and his mother are now doing the same. I suppose she has always been a little critical of me. Of the way I look. Oh, she says it kindly, but . . . ' I put my hands to my face. 'No!'

'Yes. Say it, Hetty. Because it's the only way I know that you can be saved. Say what you really feel for Cora.'

I felt the anger rising within me and realised I had been suppressing it for a very long time. 'She never lets me be myself. She has always been prettier and cleverer, and everyone has always cared more for her than they do for me. My aunts. My husband and his mother prefer her company to mine. Even Mama and Papa made more of Cora than they did of me. Perhaps that was why I . . . Oh God, Max. Why did you make me say these things? Why?'

'Because I needed you to face the truth,' he said.

Here it is: the truth that I told Max the day before I was brought to the asylum.

I hate Cora.

From the Notes of Dr Fielding

This explains much of the patient's behaviour. She has long been jealous of her more beautiful and intelligent cousin. It is possible that the patient killed her parents because she knew they preferred Miss Cora.

But what of her husband? He and Miss Cora were enemies. Unless . . . Yes, I think I see it clearly now. Their antipathy turned to love, as Sir George realised that he had an angel under his roof more exciting and desirable than his hysterical young wife. It makes me wonder if it is all a delusion after all. Has Miss Cora once again protected her cousin from the horrible truth?

I am glad to say this is no longer my problem. Let it not be said that I have harboured a criminal under my roof, especially as I have not been paid for some time. Today the patient will be taken to the public asylum, and from there she can be arrested for any crimes she has committed.

7

Testimony of Nan Bradley

I went to work at Marsholm Manor when I was twelve years old. To begin with, I helped in the kitchens. We had comfortable beds to sleep in and good food, but not much time to ourselves. It was hard work, over long days, even though the Marshes were better than most employers. I'd come from the Home Farm, where my mother was busy with all my brothers and sisters. My starting work left her one less mouth to feed, and my wage, small as it was, helped toward the family finances.

One day I was walking down the back stairs when I heard Miss Hetty crying. She would have been about four years old at the time. It wasn't long after Miss Cora came to live at the manor house. As I didn't hear any adults around, I went back upstairs to the nursery floor. It was possible that the little girl's nanny, Miss Ivy, had gone downstairs to get a cup of tea, so I decided I would wait with Miss Hetty until her nanny returned.

When I opened the door to the nursery, I was met with the horrible sight of Miss Cora, who was ten at the time, squeezing hard on Miss Hetty's plump little arms, making the little girl squeal.

'Miss Cora!' I called out to her. She turned to face me, her eyes dark with anger.

'Get out,' she said.

'You leave that little girl alone now,' I said. I folded my arms to make it plain I wasn't going anywhere.

'You get out or I'll tell my aunt that you're a thief.'

'Tell her what you want,' I said. 'I'm waiting here till Miss Ivy gets back.'

She stormed off in a huff, and I went and picked up Miss Hetty. Her brown eyes were wet with tears.

'There now,' I said. 'It's all right.' I sat down on a chair and picked up a storybook. No doubt I'd be in trouble for being late back to the kitchen, but I wasn't going to leave the little one until Miss Ivy came back.

I didn't worry too much about Miss Cora's behaviour. I had five brothers and four sisters, and when we were little we were always pinching each other or pulling each other's hair when our old mum wasn't looking. Then we'd blame the other one for starting it.

I was reading a fairy tale to Miss Hetty, who had started to doze in my lap, when Miss Ivy came back with a face like thunder. 'Much trouble you've got me into,' she said. 'The mistress wants to see you. In future, I'll thank you to keep your nose to yourself.'

I handed Miss Hetty to Miss Ivy and went downstairs to the mistress's sitting room. I fully expected to be dismissed, as Miss Cora had threatened, and I was already working out how I could explain it to my mum.

'Come on in, Anne,' said the mistress. I remember Mrs Charlotte Marsh as a very lovely woman. Miss Hetty looks a lot like her. On that day Mrs Marsh was sitting by the fire, wearing a pretty summer dress with a shawl. Sometimes I dreamed of owning a dress like that. Not that I had ideas above my station. I just used to think it would be nice to be able to wear something other than my apron.

'I'm mostly called Nan, ma'am.'

'Very well, I'll call you Nan. Sit down.'

I looked for the least important-looking chair, only for Mrs Marsh to point me to a chair opposite hers at the fire. 'I mustn't, ma'am,' I protested. There were strict rules about where servants could and could not sit. Even when the family were away, we did not break these rules, so entrenched were they into the servants' code.

'Of course you must. Sit down, please. Would you like a cup of tea, Nan?'

Well I'd never known anything like it. Servants just didn't get to drink tea with their employers. I wish to this day

I'd said yes, if only for the pleasure of drinking from such a pretty little tea set. It had pink roses on it, with a gold rim on the cup and the saucer. I was afraid I was being tested, so I refused.

'Has Miss Cora spoken to you, ma'am?' I asked when I'd sat down. 'I didn't mean any harm to the young miss, ma'am. I know what children can be like. I've got nine brothers and sisters. I just didn't want Miss Hetty to be unhappy. She's such a lovely little girl. It's so sweet the way she smiles at you and wants to be your friend, though I know it's presumptuous of me to say that.'

'I think you have been a very good friend to Miss Hetty today, Nan. That's what I wanted to talk to you about. I'm told you're a very clever girl. Cook says that you can read and write.'

'Yes, ma'am. My dad taught me. He thinks all children should have an education.'

'I happen to agree with him. Now, as to the reason I've asked to see you.

First of all, let me assure you that you are not in any trouble. As you say, children can sometimes be cruel to other children. I am sure that Miss Cora does not mean anything by it.'

It's odd, but I can still remember the doubt in the mistress's eyes when she spoke. 'Miss Ivy does need a rest sometimes. She cannot be with Miss Hetty twenty-four hours a day. So I wondered whether you would be willing to leave your work in the kitchen and move up to the nursery to help there. You'll be paid accordingly, and I'll let you read any of the books in the library. I will be relying on you to make sure there is no repeat of today's incident. Miss Hetty is not to be left alone for a moment. And if at any time you feel she might be at risk, you have my permission to step in and take her to safety. Do you understand, Nan?'

She had me at reading the books in the library. 'Yes, ma'am. At least, I think I do.'

She nodded. 'Yes, I rather think you

do. Miss Cora has had some unhappy times in her life and it sometimes makes her lash out. We just need to be sure she doesn't lash out at someone much smaller than herself, don't we?'

There was so much unsaid in that interview. So much left between the lines, as they say in the books. But it's fair to say that from that day I'd have done anything for Mrs Marsh and for Miss Hetty.

I got a lot of joshing from the kitchen staff about my promotion, most of it good-natured, but not all of it. But moving upstairs I got to see a lot of things I'd missed downstairs.

I loved the mistress and Miss Hetty, and whilst I wasn't as close to the master, I always thought he was a good man.

I also saw the Marshes make a lot of mistakes. They did it for the best of reasons, but it turned bad for them in the end.

Miss Cora, as the mistress had said, had come from an unhappy back-ground. Because of this, they went out of their way to make her happy. They bought her everything she wanted, and they praised her to the hilt. This only made her want more and demand more attention. While this was all going on, Miss Hetty was pushed aside. I don't think they meant to do it. It just happened, because Miss Cora demanded so much of their time.

I'm a great believer that people such as Mr and Mrs Marsh lead by example, so not only did the servants rally around Miss Cora every time she stamped her pretty little foot, but so did the two Miss Marshes — Molly and Dolly.

I know that the mistress and the master loved Miss Hetty. I cannot speak for the two Miss Marshes, but Miss Cora had a way of pushing her into the shadows. They spent so much time working on Miss Cora's self-worth, they didn't have time for Miss Hetty's. The poor child was left to flounder alone much of the time. I'm sure they thought she knew she was loved, but I don't think she did know it. Sometimes it just has to be said and shown.

As for Miss Cora's self-worth, I don't think it was lacking at all. I think she's just like that Narcissus fellow I read about who looked in the river and fell in love with his own reflection. She was, and still is, incapable of loving anyone but herself, and she thinks the whole world is there to do her bidding.

When Miss Cora grew more mature, she became cleverer, and realised that by appearing to love Miss Hetty, she would earn even more praise from the family. She stopped using sly physical violence against Hetty and instead began putting her down in a way that my mum calls 'damning with faint praise', so that no one could censure her about it, because they were never quite sure if she had insulted poor Miss Hetty.

I knew, but even with my promotion I was still a servant. I did my best to be a good friend to Miss Hetty, and to soothe her when she had her night terrors — usually caused by Miss Cora playing tricks in the night — but my low status prevented us from becoming true friends. Miss Cora was happy to remind Miss Hetty of this on a regular basis.

Then came that fateful day. I can hardly remember what caused the upset. Miss Cora had been bought a new dress or bonnet. It was usually something like that which set her off. But it was not to her liking. So she had sulked for most of the day, then screamed blue murder when the mistress refused to return it. 'It was the exact one you ordered,' I heard the mistress say.

Miss Cora was always doing that — ordering something, then making a scene because it wasn't what she wanted. Like the day, years later, me and Miss Hetty went into the village to get new ribbons for a bonnet that Miss Cora had decided was not good enough for her. That was the day Miss Hetty said she met her young man, but I didn't see him.

Going back to that day years before, the whole house heard the ruckus that followed the delivery of the new dress (or bonnet). Miss Cora behaved so badly — she would have been about fifteen or sixteen at the time — that Mr Marsh, who was always the most moderate of men, lost his temper and sent her to bed without supper. He even started to make plans to have her sent away.

Poor Miss Hetty also went to bed sobbing. She tried to broker a peace between them all. I don't think she ever remembered the sly little pinches and punches Miss Cora used to give her, and she had become so used to the stealthy insults that they'd become normal to her. All Miss Hetty wanted was a happy home, but it had not really been that for a long time.

And then that night, they were found dead. The master and the mistress. Stabbed to death. It was dreadful. I'd liked them both very much, and they'd always been kind to me, and the rest of the servants. Not like some bosses are.

Oh, I know what Miss Cora tried to make it seem like. She'd have liked nothing better than for Miss Hetty to be taken away. But she forgot that Miss Hetty had friends in this house. I would never have let them take her. The same when she was taken from Lakeham Abbey to that awful sanatorium run by that quack doctor. If I'd been there, I would never have let them take Miss Hetty away.

Because the manor was entailed away, we went to the hunting lodge. Well, some of us did. Me, the cook and a couple of other maids.

I'm not surprised Miss Hetty, who was about ten at the time, hated it there. It was an ugly old house with dead animals on the walls. It did nothing for poor Miss Hetty's nerves. It was also a chance for Miss Cora to torment her more often, aided by the two Miss Marshes, who were as gullible as anything. Mr and Mrs Marsh might have overindulged Miss Cora, but they had no doubt about what a scheming little minx she was. The Miss Marshes hung on her every word, and joined in with her 'faint praise' of Miss Hetty. I watched my girl become a shadow.

She even withdrew from me, which breaks my heart to this day. I know I had no claim on her friendship or affection, but I'd been with her since she was a toddler, and I wish she'd felt she could confide in me. I know why she couldn't. I know who was whispering in her ear, because as Miss Hetty grew older there were fewer excuses for me to be watching her twenty-four hours a day. It would have been overstepping the bounds.

Funnily enough, when she married, I thought she'd escaped. Sir George always seemed very polite and charming; and even though he did not look to Miss Hetty with love in his eyes, I couldn't see how he could fail to love her when they'd been together for a while. She was still labouring under the misapprehension that she was a plain girl, thanks to Miss Cora and the sisters, but anyone with eyes could see that she was every bit as beautiful as her mother.

I was glad when she went to Europe for six months, at least to begin with. Then I began to realise that Miss Cora was corresponding with Sir George. Not only that, but she was involving the servants in her subterfuge. I had no idea what was going on with her and the gentleman, but I knew that judging from her past behaviour, it would not be good. When she asked me to post a letter for her I refused, saying I would not go.

As always, she twisted it around. I should have told the Misses Marsh what had really happened, but I thought they were too stupid to understand. They made it clear what they thought of me as a servant, so I don't think it would have made any difference.

I made a mistake; I admit that now. Not about Miss Cora's strange relationship with Sir George, but in giving up my job. If I'd stayed, I might have been able to travel to Lakeham Abbey and be with Miss Hetty. Then these awful things wouldn't have happened. I can't forgive myself for not being there when she needed me.

I got a post at another house in Marsholm Cells, as a maid-companion to an elderly woman called Miss Bridges. She said that Mrs Marsh had always spoken highly of me, so she didn't care what had happened with Miss Cora. Sadly, she died a couple of years later. I found out that they were hiring up at Marsholm Manor again. It's a bit complicated, but the old Duke of Marsholm had died, and his successor was coming back from abroad. But the successor of the Duke of Marsholm was also the one to whom Marsholm Manor had been entailed, and he had decided to make that his home instead of the duke's seat near to London.

Most of the old staff had either found new posts or had passed away in the eleven years since the deaths of Mr and Mrs Marsh. But I was still surprised to be offered the job of housekeeper by the duke's right-hand man, Samuel Cooper. It was because I told Samuel all about Miss Hetty that the duke became involved. At the time I thought it was just because he felt guilty that he had not done more for her after her parents died, but I learned there was more to it than that. But that is not for me to discuss, and I'll leave His Grace to fill in those parts of the story.

We all took steps to find out about Miss Hetty, and that was how we learned she was very unhappy, and that Miss Cora had moved in with her again. It was no accident that the one circumstance coincided with the other. We all began to fear for her safety, so we investigated Sir George and his mother — and what we found out was shocking.

8

Testimony of Samuel and Nan Bradley
(as told by Nan Bradley)

Finding out about Sir George was proving to be a bit difficult for Samuel and me. Then it turned out that a villager near to Lakeham Abbey was happy to share information with us, at a cost.

'Sir George's father was a gambler,' said Miss Trent. She was an elderly spinster who had rooms above a local shop. 'Spent the family fortune in no time. So the Dowager Lady Lakeham had to take Master George to the continent. That must have been about thirty years ago. We didn't see them again until last year, when Sir George married and brought his new bride to the abbey.'

'Have you seen the new Lady

Lakeham?' I asked.

'Hardly ever,' said Miss Trent. 'We saw their carriage arriving from the honeymoon, and I think I glimpsed a pleasant young face looking out, but that was it. They don't socialise around here. We've all tried leaving visiting cards and invitations, but they're ignored. Sometimes that cousin of theirs — Miss Cora Marsh, I think her name is — will come down to the village to post a letter or buy ribbons from the haberdasher's. But she's a stuck-up little madam and won't even pass the time of day with anyone.'

She took a sip of the weak tea she had made, though the aroma from hers suggested that it drew strength from some other quarter. 'I saw the dowager a few weeks ago. At least I think it was her. It's been that long since she was at Lakeham Abbey, we've all forgotten what she looks like. She's looking well for her age, I'll give her that . . . considering the life she's led.'

'What do you mean by that?' I asked.

'Well, I am not one to gossip about such things.'

'Of course not.' I didn't point out that she was already gossiping.

'Is there anyone who can tell us more?' Samuel asked. 'Someone who might have been close to them?'

'There's old Mrs Potter, who lives in a cottage on the estate. She was the housekeeper to Sir George's mother and father when they lived abroad, and the only servant still with them. They dismissed all the original servants when they went to France, and set on all new ones when they returned, bringing Mrs Potter with them. A funny lot, they are. The servants, I mean. They don't talk to you either. And some of the men have been seen in an inebriated state in the local inns. I myself never touch liquor.' Miss Trent looked heavenward as if for confirmation. 'Apart from a small sherry at night, which my doctor tells me is conducive to a good night's sleep.'

There was little more she could tell

us, so we left her with enough money to buy several bottles of sherry and went about finding Mrs Potter.

The cottage we found was in even worse state than those on the Marsholm estate had been before the duke's renovations, and that was saying something.

I was expecting a frail old woman, so was surprised when the door was answered by a large lady with arms almost as strong as Samuel's. She was old, maybe in her seventies, but she still looked to be as strong as an ox.

'What do want?'

'Hello, Mrs Potter. I'm Nan . . . ' I paused, afraid of giving my real name in case Miss Cora should hear of it. She might have heard about me from Miss Trent, but I doubted it, given that the people at Lakeham Abbey didn't socialise in the village.

'Cooper. Mr and Mrs Cooper,' Samuel said. 'We're looking for work around here and wondered if you knew of anything at Lakeham Abbey.'

I'll say something for Samuel: he was quick at telling lies. I hadn't decided then whether that was a good thing or not.

'There's nothing doing.' Mrs Potter went to close the door, but Samuel had somehow managed to put his foot there. He held up a few pieces of silver and Mrs Potter's disinterest disappeared in an instant.

'Just a bit of information,' he said. 'We were thrown out of our last place. Not that we'd done anything wrong. After all, what servants don't sometimes try a bit of the master's wine?'

I was mortified. I'd never stolen from my employers. 'Poor Nan here is still embarrassed about it, aren't you, my darling?' Samuel put his arm around my shoulder, and it was all I could do not to shrug him off. He was getting much too familiar for my liking. 'One silly mistake and here we are.'

'Come in, but don't wake my mother.'

'Mother?' Samuel mouthed to me,

when Mrs Potter's back was turned as she lifted a pan of hot water from the fireplace.

'She must be a hundred,' I mouthed back, stopping as Mrs Potter spun around to look at us suspiciously.

'What's that you say?'

'She said that the abbey must need a hundred people to run it,' Samuel said smoothly.

'Not that many. The family don't live in all the rooms, so they've got a skeleton staff at the moment. People they trust that they brought back from the continent with them. So I don't think you've much hope of getting a place there.' She sniffed and wiped her nose on her sleeve.

I made the quick decision that I didn't like or trust Mrs Potter. She wasn't like any housekeeper I'd ever worked for. Those ladies had some refinement, usually because they were the daughters of the upper working classes or because they'd worked their way through the servant hierarchy and had all their rough spots knocked off on the journey.

I know it sounds snobbish, but Mrs Potter reminded me more of a barmaid. The cottage wasn't as tidy as it could have been, either. Most of the servants I knew kept their own homes spotless. Hard work was ingrained into them and they hated anything out of place.

She handed us a couple of grubby cups of tea and sat down. 'Who've you worked for before?' she asked.

'The Duke of Marsholm,' said Samuel without hesitation. I wanted to kick him at first. That was too close for comfort, but Mrs Potter showed no signs of making a connection with Miss Hetty.

'Really? A duke. I bet you've got lots of stories about him.'

'Oh, the things I could tell you.' Samuel winked. 'But I won't. Not till I know you better.'

I couldn't believe it. He was flirting with her. And he was supposed to be married to me!

'Tell us about Lakeham Abbey,' he said. As he spoke, he jingled a purse full of money on his lap. 'Who would we be doing for?'

'Sir George, his mother, his wife and their young cousin, Miss Marsh.'

'Just come back from abroad, haven't they?'

'What of it?'

'No, I just wondered.'

'They've been back a couple of years, actually, though Sir George went off with his new wife again for six months whilst we got things ready here.'

'House in a state, hey?'

'The whole place is. I thought with her bringing her money with her, things would change, but he's still paying off his father's gambling debts. Thousands, they were. More money than most of us make in a lifetime.' Mrs Potter clamped her lips shut, as if she realised she had said too much. 'So we just had to make do. Shift the furniture around and put the nicest we could in the best rooms. You know.'

'Yes, we know,' I said. We'd had much the same to do at Marsholm Manor when the duke moved in, but he at least had started proper renovations to the rest of the house and the estate. I didn't share any of this with Mrs Potter. I didn't want to talk too much about the duke. 'It's a hard job,' I added.

'You're telling me. Especially as there were only a couple of us to do it till this new lot arrived.'

'We've heard they like a good time,' said Samuel. He said it as though he approved.

'Well who doesn't?' Mrs Potter said coquettishly. I seethed. She was in her seventies, for goodness sake. A woman of that age had no business flirting with my pretend husband.

'Where do people go for enjoyment around here?' he asked.

'Just the local inn, the Flying Horse. Used to be there'd be barn dances on the estate, but no one's been building any barns for a long time. There's all that farmland going to waste too. Sir

George could make a fortune off that if he'd a mind to point some of that money in that direction.'

'His father was a rum 'un, then?'

She sniffed and shrugged. 'To be honest, I hardly had time to know him. He died a few months after I became their housekeeper. I was in the south of France, working, when I met Her Ladyship. The Dowager Lady Lakeham, that is. I did a favour for her and we took a fancy too each other, so she asked me to go run their villa. They wanted someone who was un-shockable. Oh the parties those two had in those days. Wild, they were, by English standards. They're all like that out there, the expats. They think no one's watching, but a clever person can benefit from that.' She tapped her nose, all the while keeping her eyes on Samuel's purse.

It occurred to me that she was talking about blackmail. What sort of people was Miss Hetty involved with? I hated to think of her being drawn into that type of society. She didn't have the temperament for it. Sir George had seemed charming enough, if you liked that sort of thing, but what if he was as debauched as his parents?

'What happened to Sir Tristan Lakeham?' I asked.

'Hanged himself, didn't he? Because of the debt. That left Lady Pamela destitute. I helped her where I could, to sell all her jewellery, but she and young Sir George hardly had anything, so he couldn't come back here and claim the estate.'

'How did they survive?'

'They had friends. Some of them were of the fair-weather kind, and disappeared when the money did. But a young couple they knew helped them as much as they could, until Sir George was old enough to take care of things himself.'

'Who were this young couple?' I asked. 'We were told that the Lakehams kept themselves to themselves and had no friends hereabouts.'

Mrs Potter opened her mouth then

shut it again. 'I think I've told you too much, considering you're only looking for a job. What did you come here for, asking all these questions? I ought to tell Sir George.'

'Go ahead,' said Samuel. 'But you've told us nothing that isn't the truth and available for all to know. I mean, if we went to the south of France, people who knew them would remember, wouldn't they?'

'Well, yes, I suppose that's true.' Mrs Potter looked relieved. Samuel took some coins from his purse and put them on the table. 'For the tea,' he said. 'And if you hear of any jobs going, let us know. We're staying at the Flying Horse tonight at least.'

As we were leaving, there came a sudden ruckus from upstairs in the cottage.

'Hush now, mother,' Mrs Potter called. 'I'll bring your tea in a minute.'

'Mother? You dare call me mother? I want to go home!'

Mrs Potter, noticing we had stopped,

made a circular gesture next to her head and said, 'Poor thing doesn't know who I am nowadays.' She called up the stairs. 'You are home, dear. Remember we talked about it?' She looked to us and tutted, as if to say, 'See how it is?'

'I wonder who the young couple were,' I said as Samuel and I walked back to the town. 'She seemed not to want to talk about them.'

'I got that impression too. I reckon it's time we went to the south of France. If Sir George and his mother have only been back here for two or three years, someone there may know them better. I'll contact the Boss and make arrangements to book a passage.'

'I can't go to France with you,' I protested. 'It'd be improper.'

'How do you work that out? We're two employees of the Duke of Marsholm working on something for him. You couldn't go alone, and I wouldn't be any good on my own. I never have been.'

'Is that why you attached yourself to the duke?' I asked.

'Yeah, something like that. I'd been brought up in the workhouse. No family to speak of. Or none that wanted anything to do with someone like me.'

'What do you mean, someone like you?'

'I don't know if you've noticed, Nan, but I'm not exactly white. They might not have slavery in England anymore, but if you're black, there's not much difference between slavery and the pittance that employers are willing to pay you. I'd been struggling all my life till I met the Boss on that boat. I saw that boy and I knew he'd be good for me, and that I could be good for him too. So I started calling him Boss immediately, even though he's a fair bit younger than I am. I wanted him to believe in himself. And I kept at him, until he did believe and we ended up making money so that we could both live well. Now look at him.'

'Sorry, Samuel, but you're not

146

responsible for him becoming a duke,' I laughed. I was touched by his story. Despite the fact that Samuel could seem a bit of a rogue, there was a truthfulness about him, and I could see why the duke had trusted him.

'No, but I gave him what he needed to build that house up and to walk with his head held high. It's not all one-sided, either. He gave me stuff too. Not just money — and he pays me what I'm worth, and then a bit more besides — but respect. He speaks to me like I'm his equal. I know he hated me calling him Boss at first, but that was just my way of getting him to be a leader of men. I'll never be able to do that. My upbringing won't let me.'

Without thinking, I put my arm in his. After all, we were supposed to be husband and wife. 'I think, Samuel Cooper, you could be anything you wanted to be.'

'That's what I need. A good woman to support me.'

'Don't you start your flirting with

147

me,' I chided, but secretly pleased. 'I'm not a pushover like some of those girls you know.'

'I know that, Nan. You're special, like Miss Hetty is special. That's why you care so much about her, isn't it?'

'I'm not as special as she is.'

'Did she tell you that?'

I shook my head. 'Goodness, no. She's been an angel to me. I don't just mean polite, as some ladies are when they are only being nice to servants because others are watching. She was always genuinely kind and respectful to the servants, as her late mother was. I think that, if not for Miss Cora interfering, Miss Hetty and I could have been friends in the way you and the duke are. If it's not presumptuous of me to say so.'

'One day people like us won't have to defer to people that are called our 'betters',' said Samuel. 'We'll all be equal. A man like me might even get a knighthood.'

'Don't you go talking like one of

those socialists,' I said, horrified. 'I know my place.'

Samuel laughed at that. 'As if anyone would ever call you downtrodden, Nan. I don't know what you do to others, but you scare me to death.'

'Do I?' My heart dropped. I'd hoped he liked me a bit, but if I scared him, that couldn't be possible. 'I don't mean to.'

He stopped and turned to face me. 'Don't change, Nan. Not for me, not for anyone. I've already told you, you're special.'

'We could go to France, I suppose,' I agreed, thinking that it might be nice to spend more time with him. 'But there's to be no funny business.'

'I wouldn't dare, Boss,' Samuel said, laughing.

'Are you doing that thing to me now?' I asked.

'What thing?'

'The thing where you think calling me Boss will make me feel better about myself?'

'Maybe. Is that a problem?'

'Not at all,' I replied. 'Let's go to the south of France . . . Boss.'

The duke seemed more than happy for us to go to the South of France, and he insisted on paying for all our travel and accommodation, along with any other money we might need for information.

For once in my life, I was glad I wasn't a great lady. If I was, I'd never have been allowed to travel alone with Samuel. Only noble ladies need chaperones. As a servant, I could go where I wanted with whoever I wanted. I also had the freedom of not having to care for anyone but myself, so I could enjoy the voyage and the train journey south.

We stopped in Paris first, because Samuel said everyone ought to see it. It is a beautiful city, and the Eiffel Tower is splendid. We went to Montmartre, which was a bit wild for my liking, though Samuel obviously enjoyed the dancing girls. They showed a bit too much leg if you ask me. But the music was exciting and after a while I could not help tapping my feet.

In the evening we walked along the Seine, but I felt a little uncomfortable, despite the pretty lights along the river and the gentle lap of the water against the bank. 'What are we doing, Samuel?' I asked.

'We're walking along the river.'

'I know that. What I mean is, what are we doing *here?* We're supposed to be helping Miss Hetty, yet it seems like we're on holiday.'

'You looked after her for a long time, didn't you?'

'You already know the answer to that. I've cared for her since I was twelve and I stopped that little madam from hurting her. But it's not just that. I'm used to being a servant and doing for others. What would His Grace think if he knew we were wasting his money here?'

'We're not. My money has paid for this little jaunt. As for His Grace, he'd be glad you're having a rest. Nan?'

'Yes?'

'What will you do if we manage to get Miss Hetty away?'

'What do you mean?'

'Will you go back to caring for her?'

'I suppose so. I hadn't thought of it. But yes, if she wants me to, I will. I'm not sure how we left things, because of the way Miss Cora lies and schemes. She mightn't want to know me.'

'So you're happy to be a servant all your life?'

'It's what I was born to.'

'But it wasn't, Nan. You can do anything you want to do. You can read and write, for a start, which is more than I can do.'

'But you can build things, Samuel. Beautiful things. I've seen the pictures of His Grace's home in the colonies. And what you've done to Marsholm Manor.'

'We're not talking about me,' he protested. 'We're talking about you. Chances are that Miss Hetty might want to marry again, and she may not need someone to take quite as much care of her as you did. I should hope not, anyway. It would be a sorry thing if the girl left her husband and the evil Miss Cora only to marry an abusive man. Not that I think that'll happen. I think His Grace has something up his sleeve. She'll probably marry and have children.'

'I certainly hope not — at least, not too soon. She's not a brood mare, you know. And anyway, she may not be able to divorce.'

'That depends on what we find out about Sir George. We might be able to persuade him to let her go.'

'So the sooner we get to the south of France the better. This goes back to my earlier question — what are we doing here, Samuel?'

'We're having a nice time, because I thought you'd like to see Paris. Because I thought you'd like to spend time with me. But all you think about is Miss Hetty. Miss Hetty this. Miss Hetty that.'

'She's the reason we're here!'

'Yes, I know. But sometimes I just

wish you'd think of . . . oh, never mind.'
He walked on ahead, leaving me
standing there, puzzled.

'That's not very gentlemanly,' I said.
'Leaving me alone in the dark.'

'I'd pity any man who tried to take
you on, Nan.'

'I'm not that hardened, am I,
Samuel? I don't mean to be. It's like I
told you. I was twelve when I first
started caring for her, no more than a
child myself. I've had to be tough to
survive in that house, with all the
intrigue and scheming. I've had to
stand my ground so many times, to the
point that I'm exhausted by it all. But it
doesn't mean my heart isn't there, and
nor does it mean I'm incapable of
loving anyone but Miss Hetty.' I took a
deep breath. Tears stung my eyes. 'But
you're just teasing me anyway, aren't
you? I know your reputation. Maybe I
have to be tough with you too, so that
I don't end up with my heart broken.'

He walked back to me. 'That's the
most honest I've ever heard you be

about your life,' he said. He stroked my cheek. 'Mrs Marsh asked a hell of a lot of you, Nan, given that you were so young. I'm not sure she should have expected you to shoulder such a burden.'

'She was desperate, I think. And I'd do it all again.'

'I know you would, and that's why you're different from any other woman I know. It's why I wanted to bring you to Paris. Because if anyone deserves something good happening to them, it's you, Nan Bradley.'

He kissed me then, though I'm sure that's not really important to this investigation. I don't even know why I've put it. Perhaps I should cross it out before His Grace reads it. I'm sure he wouldn't appreciate us carrying on such shenanigans when we were on a sacred mission to find out the truth. It was a very nice kiss, though, and the first I'd ever known. So perhaps that's why I feel I should mention it.

We left for Monte Carlo the next day. I must admit I preferred the south of

France to Paris. The sea glowed like a sapphire, and the villas were all bright and white, with pretty flowers in all the gardens, most of which I couldn't even name.

'You could build villas here, Samuel,' I suggested. 'I bet there's a living to be made.'

'Maybe. I'm busy at the moment working for the Boss. Anyway, why would I want to leave Marsholm?' He smiled at me. 'Unless I could bring you with me.'

'I hope you're not suggesting we live in sin, Samuel.'

'The Boss would throttle me. He's already warned me to be good to you. So marriage it would have to be.'

'Don't let me force you,' I said, walking off in a huff. I was secretly pleased that His Grace had cared about my honour.

'Nan, you really are the most exasperating woman. I've just proposed to you and you take umbrage.'

'You only proposed because His

Grace warned you about me.'

'I'd already decided to propose five minutes after I met you and before I told the Boss about you.'

I stopped and turned back to him, holding out my hand. 'Well that's all right, then.'

I felt a bit shy, being in France and not speaking the language, but Samuel had a way of ignoring all that and steaming his way into people's lives. Just as he had into my life and the duke's, in fact.

I'd been sure it was going to be difficult to find out anything, but on the first day Samuel spoke to a man who worked in a boatyard, who knew someone who worked at the casino, who knew someone else that used to work at the Lakehams' villa.

'The expat community here is pretty small,' he explained to me. 'Everyone knows everyone else. They all attend the same soirées and balls. The English-speaking servants stick together too. The woman we're going to see was a governess to Sir George. She married a local and stayed here.'

The woman, Mrs Louisa Buchet, and her husband, Pierre, owned a small café high on a clifftop. For the life of me I couldn't understand why people wanted to go that far just for a cup of coffee or glass of red wine, but it seemed to be the thing to do.

For a few minutes we sat with a glass of wine, enjoying the view. I have to admit I could see the appeal from that vantage point. The sea glistened below us and the town looked like something from a picture book or a miniature village.

'It'd be nice living here,' said Samuel as we drank our wine. 'Seeing that view every day. Maybe helping people to build their villas. I think I'd like that.'

'What's it like in the colonies?'

'Lazy,' he said. 'But in the best possible way. The days go on forever and no one rushes, except the English. They rush everywhere when they first arrive, just like the Boss did. But the natives don't. They know they have all the time in the world. Eventually the English slow down too, as they become more used to the rhythm of the place.'

'Why did you go there, Samuel?'

'It's where my father came from. So I'm told. He was a sailor. I suppose I hoped I'd find him, but I didn't.' He laughed softly. 'I wouldn't really know where to start. I found the Boss instead. He's become my family. And so have you now.' He put his hand over mine. I drew it away, not really minding, but feeling shy, because I could see we were being watched by a woman from the door. I still bore the blush of last night's kisses on my cheeks and his touch reminded me of that.

'Is that Madame Buchet?' I asked. She looked about fifty-five years of age, with dyed red hair and thick rouge on her cheeks.

Samuel turned. '*Bonjour*,' he said to her. 'Nice place you have here.'

'I am glad you think so, monsieur.'

I decided it couldn't be Madame

Buchet because the woman affected a French accent.

'Business good?' asked Samuel.

'*Oui.*'

'We're thinking of buying a place out here,' he lied. 'Is it worth it?'

'You are opening a café?' The woman's eyes narrowed.

'No, nothing like that. Don't worry. I'm a builder.'

'There is always work here for builders, monsieur.' The woman moved forward, as taken with Samuel's charm as every woman I had ever seen in his company. 'The English come, but don't like the French plumbing, or they want their drawing rooms and libraries to resemble those they left behind.' The more she spoke, the more I realised that her French accent was put on. It wasn't a bad attempt, but it wasn't perfect.

'That's what I thought,' he said. 'I did some work here, oh a few years ago now, for the Lakehams. Do you know them?'

'I used to work for them too, but I do

not remember you, monsieur.'

'It might have been after your time. When did you leave them?'

'I was governess to their boy, George, until he was fifteen years old, so it would have been about thirty years ago.'

'Sir George? Yes, I know him. He was a grown-up when I did some work for them. Is he still here?'

'They left a couple of years ago, to return to England. Or so I heard.'

'I bet you could tell me some stories about them,' said Samuel.

She tutted. 'I am not one for gossip, monsieur.'

'No, of course not. Shall we have another bottle of wine, Nan?' he asked me, as if her response was of no matter to him. 'Something expensive.'

'It all tastes like vinegar to me,' I muttered.

'Try the white,' he suggested. 'It's not as heavy.'

'I'm gasping for a cup of tea.'

'Now that I can get you,' said

Madame Buchet, who suddenly seemed to warm to me. 'Some of the English ladies prefer it. Wine for you, monsieur?'

'Why not?' said Samuel.

She returned a short time later with a pot of tea for me, with handmade biscuits, and wine for Samuel.

'Why don't you bring another cup and join us?' I suggested. 'There's no one else here and you look like you could do with a rest.'

'I reckon I will,' she agreed, dropping the French accent. She brought her cup and slumped down in the chair. 'Oh, it's so nice to drop the airs and graces. The expats like to hear an accent so they know they're really in France. I've got good at it, but it's hard some days, especially when I'm tired.'

'Did you know Mrs Potter when you worked for the Lakehams?' I asked after we'd spent ten minutes chatting about the business and difficult customers. 'Samuel has told me some right stories about her.' I prayed that she wouldn't question me about what stories, but it seemed that knowing of the woman's reputation was enough.

'Did I ever? She came to them while I was there. A housekeeper, she was supposed to be, but she'd never done any housekeeping. She just used it as an excuse to shout at the French maids. One of them, Cecily, was my husband's sister. That's how we met. The poor girl used to come crying to me about how poorly treated she was by Potter. There's a lot that happened in that house I disapproved of, but I liked the child. He was a bit under his mother's thumb, and that of his cousins, who were regular visitors, but he wasn't a bad child.'

'Yes, we were told something about the cousins, weren't we, Samuel?' I was a bit shocked to realise that I was becoming as good a liar as him. 'Or was that just the friends?'

'They were both, cousins and friends. Or kissing cousins, as we used to call them. And them with a little girl still in the cradle.'

'Kissing cousins?' Samuel sat up. 'Yeah, yeah, we heard something about that, didn't we, Nan?'

'It's like I said,' Madame Buchet continued. 'The goings on in that house. Wild parties. Couples coming and going at all hours. Or staying overnight. And they weren't all married . . . ' She lowered her voice towards the end. 'If they were married, they didn't all stay with their spouse, if you know what I mean.'

'Who were these cousins?' I asked. 'Are they still here?'

'No, they left when the Lakehams did. No, that's wrong. The little girl left years before that, when she was about ten. Her father had died, and her mother stayed on here, sending her to relatives. She was a proper little madam, that one.'

'Who was she?' I asked, even though I'd already guessed by then. I don't know why I hadn't seen the connection sooner.

'Her mother is Adeline Smith-Warren as was. She was related to the

Lakehams in some way. And her father was called Julius Marsh. Proper little madam was Miss Cora.'

9

Investigation by Nan Bradley and Samuel Cooper cont.

'Have you come to do more work on the Lakehams then?' Madame Buchet asked, not realising how her words had shocked us. 'I suppose that's why you're asking all this. Afraid of not being paid, eh?'

'Maybe,' said Samuel.

'I thought so. Because they're coming back.'

I almost opened my mouth to say, 'What?' But Samuel's warning glance stopped me.

'Yeah, they said they might be. But we don't know when.'

'In a couple of weeks. They sent word to one of the girls who used to work in their kitchens, expecting her to drop everything to join them again. They owe her wages from last time! Besides, she's with a respectable family now.'

'Is the new Lady Lakeham coming?' I asked.

Mrs Buchet smirked and raised an eyebrow. 'I imagine so. Though I don't give that much for her.' She snapped her fingers. I wanted to slap her, talking about Miss Hetty like that.

'You don't like her?' I said. 'How can you say that if you've never met her?'

'Of course I've met her. Oh, you'll have to excuse me, customers are coming.' She got up, leaving us wondering what she was on about. She could not have met Miss Hetty, unless Sir George brought her to France on their honeymoon, and I felt sure that he had not.

As we seemed to have come to the end of any investigation there, we walked back down to the town.

'That little minx, Miss Cora, worked it all out,' I said to Samuel. 'She pushed Miss Hetty into marrying Sir George, and I bet it was because of the money.

And now people are judging that poor innocent girl because of him and his family.'

'It definitely sounds as if Sir George and his mother were on their uppers.'

'Not only that, but when Miss Cora arrived at Marsholm Manor, Mr and Mrs Marsh were told her mother and father had died. It's like this has been planned all along, Samuel. But how could it be? How could Miss Cora have known that Mr and Mrs Marsh would die in such a horrible way . . . ' I put my hands to my mouth. What I was thinking seemed impossible. 'Do you think she might have let the killers in?'

'Is that what you're thinking?' Samuel asked. He had a funny look on his face, like he thought I was being really stupid or something.

'Oh, I don't know,' I replied. 'She was always a scheming little wretch. From the sound of it, she was brought up with a dissolute lot an' all. What if they deliberately separated Miss Hetty from all who loved her, ready for when she was old enough to marry?'

'From what you've told me, it does sound as if Miss Cora did her best to keep Miss Hetty away from others, making out the young ladies in the area didn't like her. But Miss Cora was what, ten years old when she came to live with the Marshes? I doubt she had Miss Hetty's marriage planned then.'

'Maybe not, but she was a clever child, was Miss Cora. Tricky. And now poor Miss Hetty is trapped, married to a man who comes from a debauched background. Who knows what he might lead her into?'

We found out when we got back to the hotel. There was a message waiting for us from the duke. He said that Miss Hetty had been taken into a mental hospital. We caught the next train back.

Testimony of Henrietta Lakeham

I am undone.

I do not care anymore what happens

to me, for I clearly am as mad as they say.

Today is the day they take me to the public asylum, but that is not the reason I am distressed.

I had thought to find peace here. The assistants seemed to like me, because I caused them little trouble. I had even started to help with the other patients, and I found such work therapeutic. It made me realise how fortunate I have been in my life. No longer was I assailed by the nightmares and fears of saying and doing the wrong thing. I was very nearly happy here, but for the fact of missing Max and wondering where he was.

But that is not why I am distressed.

It happened last night. I had been for a treatment. It was one that was particularly distressing, though I had tried so hard to keep my sanity throughout it. I do not see how they say these things can help to ease a troubled mind, when they often cause even more discomfort and unease.

There was a new girl working in the lounge, where if our behaviour has been good, we are allowed to sit and read, and talk to each other. Not that anyone says much, as we are all too afraid of giving ourselves away.

But I saw the girl. She was wearing the uniform of one of the assistants, and I felt sure I knew her. She was with a black man I had not seen before. I ran to her side. 'Nan!' I cried. 'It is you.'

She looked at me with a question in her eyes — and something else I could not define — and said, 'Sorry, miss, but my name is Sarah.'

'No,' I protested. 'You are Nan. I have known you most of my life.'

'My name is Sarah. Sorry, miss. I must get on with my work.'

'No,' I protested again and again. 'You are Nan. I know you are.' I became hysterical, and the attendants taking care of me grabbed my arms. 'Let me go!' I screamed. 'Let me go!'

I do not remember much then, only that I was put into a straitjacket and dragged to my room. Dr Fielding came to see me, but I would not talk to him. He does not care about me. No one cares about me. I had thought to find an old friend and I had been wrong.

What did it mean? I wondered as I lay there. If the girl who looked so much like Nan is not Nan, then does that mean she never existed? And if Nan never existed, does that mean I imagined Max too? That I had somehow conjured up two people whom I felt were on my side against my cousin and aunts, who watched my every move? If that was so, it explained why they behaved the way she did. For I am clearly deranged.

I have been waiting every day for my love to come and find me, but he will not, because he does not exist. What else have I imagined? What else have I done that I have forgotten? Is it possible I did the terrible thing of which I am accused?

I am akin to Penelope's tapestry. Every day, as I have waited for him, I have become whole. When the truth of my situation becomes apparent in the dark of the night, I unravel.

Now I am completely undone.

Testimony of Samuel Cooper and Nan Bradley (cont)

When we learned that Miss Hetty had been taken away, we were all worried. When we found her, we were horrified to learn she was with that quack, Dr Fielding. He had already been in the papers about some dodgy treatments given to society ladies, yet still he was able to oversee St Jude's.

It took a while, but finally I was able to acquire a post there, as did Samuel. We were employed as ward assistants and more easily than we thought we'd be. As Samuel said, 'All the reading up we've done on mental illness, and all we needed to be able to do was walk and scratch our behind at the same time.'

We had to bide our time, so we kept

out of Miss Hetty's way as much as possible. It wasn't too difficult. She kept to her room a lot and we were always busy doing other things when she was taken for her treatment.

Many of the other workers — I refuse to call them nurses — drank to excess. I'd have sympathy for them, given the sadness they have to deal with every day, but they were often brutish and violent to the patients. I think the only reason Miss Hetty escaped being harmed was because she was so docile.

The patients were a sorry bunch. There was one young lady who'd been sent there because she'd had a child out of wedlock. Dr Fielding said it was a sign of her being deranged or something. When I talked to her about her life, and the awful man that had moved in with her mother after her father's death, I learned differently. That poor child was being punished for someone else's crime.

Whilst the public rooms, where people came to visit patients, were elegant and clean, the rest of the place was badly kept. Even the servants' quarters at Marsholm Manor were cleaner and more comfortable than the bedrooms the patients had to sleep in.

'Miss Hetty shouldn't be here,' I said to Samuel on more than one occasion as we went about our work.

'We'll get her out,' he promised.

'Yes, but when?' We kept waiting for the right time, but it never seemed to come.

Then she saw me. It was bad enough that she looked so drawn and ill. I hated lying to her, and seeing her lovely face crumple when I denied who I was. If it's not blasphemous to say so, I know how St Peter felt now, and I thought that if I could be crucified upside down, it was no less than I deserved. I'd let Miss Hetty down before and as far as she could see, I was letting her down again.

That night the chance we'd been waiting for came. Kitty, one of the attendants, came to my room, complaining. She was a sixteen-year-old girl of low intelligence, who often slapped and pinched the patients. She used to work in service, but had been thrown out for stealing, though she denied it. No matter what she'd done, she'd no business being a nurse to anyone.

'They've said I've got to take Her Ladyship to the municipal asylum,' she said, slumping down on my bed without being asked. 'I hate going there. It's not nice, like here.'

I didn't respond to that, but I supposed that the municipal asylum wouldn't even bother with nice rooms for the visitors, let alone the patients. 'Which lady?' I asked. There were quite a few there.

'Lady Lakeham. You know, the quiet, stupid one.'

I almost protested, but said nothing.

'I don't want to go,' Kitty moaned. 'I'd tell his nibs where to go, but I need the job. I suppose I could take Lenny with me for protection.'

I shuddered at that thought. Lenny worked in the stables, but often came around the house, leering at the young ladies. I didn't like that one bit.

'Tell you what,' I said. 'Why don't I take her, with Samuel? You can have the night off.' I added, for good measure, 'With Lenny.'

Her dull eyes lit up. 'What about the doctor?'

'He won't be there. He never is when patients get sent on elsewhere.' It was guilt, pure and simple, but I didn't tell Kitty that. She was liable to go and repeat what I'd said.

'All right, that's what we'll do,' said Kitty. She kissed my cheek, which was a bit more familiar than I was accustomed to. 'I really like you. I knew we'd be friends the first time I saw you.'

I doubted that very much, as I'd once overheard Kitty telling everyone that I put on airs and graces and thought myself as good as the gentlewomen patients, but I smiled back anyway.

As soon as I could, I went to Samuel and told him that our chance had come. 'You have to work out a way to redirect the coach,' I told him.

'Don't worry, Nan. I'll do it, even if I have to knock out the driver.'

'Samuel, please don't go getting into trouble,' I said.

The coach was coming at seven o'clock that evening. Kitty had told me that the municipal asylum, which was about two hours away, liked to take new patients at night, whilst all the others were sleeping, so as not to cause any disturbance.

I managed to arrange with one of the more sensible attendants to give Miss Hetty a sedative beforehand. It was not something I would have trusted to Kitty, who would no doubt have ended up killing my girl.

Just before seven, me and Samuel went into her room to find her sleeping. 'Poor love,' I said, stroking her hair. She looked so sweet and innocent lying there. I wanted to cry for all the wrong that had been done to her, but there was no time for sentiment.

'Come on,' I said to Samuel. 'Let's

get her out of this place.'

He lifted her into his arms so gently I thought I would cry again. He'd no reason to help me, not really. Only the fact that he was — and still is — a good man who cares about the things I care about.

We were nearly at the front door when Dr Fielding stopped us. I couldn't believe our bad luck. He never came to see patients off.

'Just on my way out,' he said, even though we'd asked for no explanation and he didn't have to give us one. He was staggering slightly and I could smell brandy on his breath. That was nothing new either. His complexion was florid and his eyes watery. 'What are you two doing?'

'Taking Miss . . . Lady Lakeham to the municipal asylum, sir,' I said.

'Oh yes . . . I thought Kitty was doing it, with Lenny.'

'She was sir, but there was a problem with one of the patients going a bit doolally, so they're sorting that out.' I knew he would never go to check on that patient. He was never around when patients actually needed him, and from what I'd found out, he was only interested in Miss Hetty for as long as Miss Cora kept coming to visit.

'Yes, best leave it to them. Go on then, get the baggage out of here, and come back straight away. I don't know why the other place can't send their own people.'

'Yes sir,' I said, wanting to slap him for calling Miss Hetty 'baggage'. I heard Samuel breathe in sharply and I knew that was what he'd expected me to do.

We rushed out into the yard and put Miss Hetty in the waiting coach, then we climbed in after her. I didn't breathe properly till we were half an hour down the road. I kept expecting to be stopped. It was a relief to know we'd never have to go back to that awful place. We just had to make sure that we redirected the coach so that Miss Hetty didn't end up in the municipal asylum.

It was a frosty night, so I wrapped

Miss Hetty in a blanket and sat next to her to make sure she did not fall as the coach set off, rolling over the rocky ground.

'You really love her, don't you?' asked Samuel.

'I've known her since she was four years old. I've seen that . . . that witch, Miss Cora, play with her poor young mind and encourage those two silly sisters to join in with the torment. Yet through it all, Miss Hetty has always been gentle and kind to all she meets. She's a lot stronger than she thinks, but I'm afraid of what that doctor has done to her in that awful place. When I think of people like Kitty allowed to care for the afflicted . . . it makes me furious!'

'Why do you think the duke has helped us so much? He doesn't even know her.'

'I don't know. Maybe he thinks that the previous duke neglected the family for long enough. She'll be happy back at Marsholm. She'll have time to heal and maybe someday she can put all this behind her.' I lowered my voice. 'Have you thought about how you're going to sort out the driver?'

'Don't worry. It's all in hand.'

We had been travelling for over an hour when Samuel knocked on the roof. 'Driver, stop.' He stood up, as much as he could in the low coach, and put his head out through the window. 'There's a coaching inn not far from here. Stop there and we'll take some refreshment.'

The driver said, 'I'm told I've got to get on and straight back.'

'I'm paying,' said Samuel.

There was a pause. The driver was probably thinking about it. 'Righty ho.'

We stopped at the inn about ten minutes later.

'Wait here,' Samuel said.

'What are you going to do? You're not going to hurt him, are you, Samuel?'

'No, of course not. I'm just going to buy him a drink, like I said.' Samuel winked, but it still took me a minute or two to catch on. He was going to get the coachman drunk.

I didn't think that would take too long, but it was nearly an hour before the coach door opened again, and it wasn't Samuel standing there.

'Your Grace,' I said. 'How did you know where to find us?'

'Samuel sent me a message. I've been riding all day. Come on, I've found a coach.'

Before I could say any more, he'd climbed into the coach and had picked Miss Hetty up in his arms. He gave her a really funny look. Not unkind or anything. More like wonder. And sadness.

I followed him as he carried her to another coach, making sure I'd shut the door of the one we just left. He lifted her into the new coach, which was far more comfortable than the one we'd used, and sat next to her, resting her head on his shoulder.

I must admit I felt a bit put out. It was my job to look after Miss Hetty, but I didn't say anything. After all, the duke had been helping us. He did seem to have taken to her very quickly though. I couldn't blame him. She was a beautiful young lady — even if others would have you believe otherwise.

The duke banged on the roof and the coach started, which took me by surprise. 'What about Samuel?' I asked. 'I mean, sorry, Your Grace but . . . ' It sounds daft, but I had the horrible feeling that Samuel would be taken to the asylum and kept there under lock and key because of what we'd done.

'He needs to let the other driver think you're still in the coach, and the best way to do that is to get him very drunk. As soon as he can get away, he'll follow us. I've arranged a fresh horse for him. Don't worry, Nan. I shan't let anything happen to him.'

I felt a bit silly then. The thing is, I didn't know the duke very well; and though he'd been very helpful and kind to us, I didn't quite know why. I think living in that house, with Miss Cora and the twins, I'd stopped trusting my own judgement where other people were concerned.

It was hours before we got to Marsholm Manor, and I'd fallen asleep, which I was a bit embarrassed about when we arrived at the manor. 'Sorry, Your Grace,' I muttered.

'You've had an exhausting day, Nan. There's no need to apologise.'

He lifted Miss Hetty down from the coach and carried her ever so gently up the steps to the house. She started to stir again, and was a bit more aware this time.

'Home . . . ' she whispered, looking up at the door. 'I'm home? Can this be true?'

'It's true, Miss Hetty,' I said. I know I was supposed to call her m'lady, but I couldn't admit to her being married to Sir George Lakeham. She was still my Miss Hetty and always would be.

'Nan? Is that you?' She became a little bit distressed and tried to get out of the duke's arms. 'No, it can't be. This is a dream.' She finally realised that the duke had a hold of her and went silent. He set her down gently, but kept hold of her.

'You're home, darling Hetty,' he said in a gentle voice that made me want to cry again. 'And Nan is most definitely here, as am I.'

She reached up and touched his face. 'Are you real? You feel real. But I'm not sure anymore.' He took her hand in his and kissed her palm.

'It's me, my darling, and I'm very real.'

'Oh Max,' she said, falling against his shoulder and bursting into tears.

Testimony of the Duke of Marsholm

My name is Maximilian Marsh — now the Duke of Marsholm. Until I was eighteen, I worked as a clerk in a shipping office in Essex. Every day I used to watch the ships sailing the Thames estuary. I dreamed of sailing away and making my fortune. For a short time I even considered piracy, but that was when I was fifteen. By the time I reached eighteen, I was of the mind that a man must always be honest in his dealings. I must have been an insufferable prig, but there you have it.

My father had been a theatre manager, and my mother was, and still is, an actress. She says my father died in a duel for her honour, though when she has had a lot to drink she often says ruefully that it was 'probably too late for that'. The truth was that my father died in a debtor's prison, but I have never let on to my mother that I know.

It is fair to say then that I was penniless and thought myself to be very far removed from any inheritance. To put it bluntly, on the Marsh family tree, we were mere windfalls. So it was something of a surprise when I inherited Marsholm Manor.

I would like to say that I did not take on the house over superstition due to the way Julius and Charlotte Marsholm had died, but with a dead debt-ridden father and an actress mother who was often 'resting', I had known hardship in my life and had lived in some terrible places, so I was not that fastidious. My life had been long stretches of poverty broken by occasional stretches of riches, when I was able to attend a good school, falling again to poverty when my mother's acting roles — and the interest of her protectors — dried up.

The problem was that whilst I had been left the estate of Marsholm Manor, there was no money to go with it. I could not afford to claim my inheritance, even if I had wanted to.

My mother, Celia, had the idea that I should marry Julius Marsh's daughter, Henrietta. Her money, when she came of age, would have helped me to run the estate, and my offer would ensure she did not become homeless. After all, my mother told me, Miss Henrietta Marsh had been orphaned in the most tragic circumstances.

I will not bore you with the impassioned speech I made to Mama about the subject. The gist of it was that I would make my own way in the world and no wife would bankroll me. I had little idea at the time how I would do this, but I was adamant that I could not live any other way.

My mother's response was, 'Have you been reading Thomas Hardy again, Max? Really, darling, he's too grim. Try Lord Byron. He's up for anything.'

She did relent a little when I pointed out that Henrietta Marsh was only ten years old at the time, and the idea of becoming engaged — however informally — to a child was ludicrous.

Nevertheless, as I grew older I became curious about Henrietta Marsh, and thought I would visit Marsholm just once to see her for myself. I must admit I felt some guilt at leaving her to flounder, though I had allowed her and her aunts and some companion or other to live in a lodge on the estate for a peppercorn rent. If I sound generous, it is an illusion. I only did so because it was cheaper than trying to maintain

Marsholm Manor. Yet there was some part of me that felt guilt at putting a girl out of her home.

When I visited the village of Marsholm Cells, I had already booked a passage to the West Indies. It was my plan to work hard for a few years then return rich enough to live the life of a gentleman.

Then I saw her. I cannot begin to tell you how beautiful she was, standing on the terrace in the moonlight. Luckily I saw her before she saw me, so I was able to compose myself and pretend nonchalance.

It was as well that no one knew who I was. I managed to slip into the ball — people were coming and going, and no one really noticed a lone man slipping in through the French doors — and watched her as she danced. I know that she mostly danced with Sir George Lakeham. I wanted to dance with her, but feared questions about who I was and why I was there. They would be sure to be asked about a man dancing with such a lovely young lady, especially one of fortune.

There was something fragile about her, but I also sensed something else — a hidden strength. I suppose I must have imagined it then, for it is only now I know how strong she has had to be.

I only saw her once more in Marsholm Cells, as I was about to leave by coach. I did not want to go, but common sense told me that a man does not throw his ambitions away for a girl he has met only twice, no matter how lovely she is.

Besides, I had nothing to offer her and I was still too proud to live off my wife's income. Impulsively, I gave her a false name — using my mother's maiden name of Parish, because I was ashamed that I had left it so long to make her acquaintance.

Now I curse that common sense and pride. I should have stayed. I might have saved her . . .

You have already been told the story of those meetings, so I will not repeat them here. Only to say that it broke my heart to leave her, despite our short acquaintance.

My adventures in the West Indies are not important to this story. Suffice to say I worked hard and eventually, after a couple of years in which I thought I would starve, I became a rich man, with a house overlooking the sea and my own small fleet of cargo ships.

It was when I arrived in the colonies that Samuel Cooper came to work for me. Well . . . that's something of an exaggeration. It's fair to say that Samuel, who was about thirty-five years of age when I first met him, attached himself to me on the voyage over. He had been an apprentice bricklayer, he said, and he was going to the colonies in the hopes of building homes for the rich landowners.

For some reason, he followed me all the way to the lodgings I had arranged, somehow managing to carry all my bags and his, despite my protestations. To be honest I thought he was using it as a ruse to steal from me, but when I

unpacked later that night before collapsing into bed, exhausted, everything
I owned — including a small amount of
money I had hidden away — was there.

Some people enter your life in
strange ways, and oddly enough, you
forget to mind their presence after a
while, even if they are rather intrusive.
Mainly because they turn out to be the
best friends you ever had. Samuel
became that for me.

After I'd tripped up over him several
times as I came out of my door in the
mornings, I invited him to live with me.
There was only one single bed in my
lodging, so we took turns sleeping in it.
Samuel knew all the angles and all the
ways to get rich legally in that part of
the world. He also knew a few illegal
ways. It took me some time to convince
him that I was not that desperate to be
rich. 'Right, Boss,' he'd say, winking.

'I really mean it, Samuel. And I'm
not your boss. I can't even pay you.'

'You can pay me when you're rich,
Boss.'

'Stop calling me Boss. My name is Max.'

'Can't do that, Boss. I'd have problems with the others if I was seen to be sidling up to the management.'

I laughed at that. 'I'm hardly that, Samuel. I can barely manage myself, let alone you.'

'Then leave it to me, Boss. I'll point you in the right direction.'

'It had better be the right direction,' I insisted. 'I'm not breaking any laws.'

'Understood, Boss.'

'Why me, Samuel? There are dozens of hungry young men here with better prospects. Why pick on me?'

'You're hungrier than any of them, Boss. I could see it in your eyes when we met on the boat.'

'If I looked hungry, it's because the rations at sea were pitiful.'

'You know what I mean, Boss. You've come here to prove something and I want to be there when you do.'

After a while, and when it was clear I was not going to get rid of him, we came to understand each other and he became my right-hand man. He was an incredible man, without the ability to read or write, but he knew figures and shapes better than anyone I had ever met. When I had earned enough money, he helped me to build my house overlooking the sea. He also built himself a cottage in the grounds, so that he was never far away from me.

I worked long hours that left me little time for socialising. Or perhaps that was just an excuse I used, because for the first few months every time I met a pretty young woman, I saw Henrietta looking back at me. Eventually that sensation faded, perhaps because those pretty young women did not want to know a penniless prospector from England. But even then, occasionally when I sat in my rooms late at night she would enter my mind unbidden. I imagined that she had married and had children, so I thought of her with a vague fondness as the road not travelled.

After all, what did I really know of her? We had spent less than ten minutes in each other's company and shared only a few words. It is not always true that absence makes the heart grow fonder. A tender shoot needs lots of attention in order for it to grow. Yet it seems now that she was always there in the background, haunting me.

There were other women. I was a young healthy male and was certainly no saint in those years. But none were the type of woman I could take home to Mother. Who am I fooling? I could probably take home any type of woman to *my* mother. Let us just say they were not the type of women I wanted to present to her.

I had been abroad four years when I received the news that I had inherited the seat of the Duke of Marsholm. I must confess I had no idea I was in line for it. Our family were, I believed, even further from the duke than Julius Marsh. The previous duke had died without issue, or closer male relatives.

Julius Marsh, who should have inherited, was dead. That left me.

I saw some irony in the situation. I had worked for several years to make a better life for myself and my mother — who had insisted on remaining in England with her 'adoring public' — and suddenly I had inherited not only the duke's palace but a substantial fortune. Money, they say, goes to money.

I decided to return home — bringing Samuel Cooper with me (I doubt he would have stayed behind) — and find out whether the palace was a suitable home in which my mother could live for the rest of her days. I had no intention of remaining in England.

I hated the palace the moment I saw it. It was decorated in a vulgar fashion and was much too big to be considered a family home. As I was in Britain, I decided to call on Marsholm Manor instead. I had only ever seen it from a distance, even though I owned it. There was something about that house when I saw it. Something that demanded love and attention. I decided that if my mother were to live anywhere, this would be the place.

I confess I had some foolish notion of making the acquaintance of Henrietta Marsh again. I think it was being there that did it. Seeing that house, and remembering that she had lived there as a child until that terrible night.

Strangely, the manor did not have the atmosphere one might associate with a building where two people had been brutally slain. Despite having plenty of rooms, it was what one might call cosy, but with a warmth that came from its previous owners. It was also falling apart.

So for the first few months of my return, Samuel and I spent all our time on renovations. Samuel also managed to shame me, in the way only a good and loyal friend can.

'Excuse me, Boss,' he said one day, when we had a meeting about the renovations. He immediately corrected himself. Coming back to England seemed to have curbed his personality somewhat, which I felt was a shame. 'I mean Your Grace. People in the village are muttering.'

'You can call me Boss, Samuel, if you insist on not calling me Max. What are they muttering about?'

'The thing is, Boss, a lot of people were put out of work when Marsholm Manor was closed up. Some of the tenant farmers have also been struggling to keep a roof over their heads.'

'I have not thrown them out, Samuel.'

'No, I don't mean that, Boss. They've literally been struggling to keep a roof over their heads. Their cottages are falling down.' His honest brown eyes met mine squarely.

I sighed. 'I see. What must they think of me, Samuel? I should have thought of this place when I made my money. I don't know what kept me away so long. Give permission for any alterations they need, and then employ some of the local women to work in the house. We have been living like a couple of tramps, but now the upstairs renovations are completed, we have servants' quarters again.'

'There is one young lady in the kitchens now, Boss. Her name is Nan. She used to work here in Mr Julius's time. She popped in to see if she could get a job.'

'I admire her initiative. Set her on, Samuel, in whatever role you think best.'

'Housekeeper, I reckon, Boss.'

'You'd already made up your mind, of course,' I said, unable to suppress a smile. 'Is she pretty?'

'She has something about her.'

'Well, behave yourself,' I chided in the way only an old friend could. 'I know your eye for the ladies. We're not in the colonies now, Samuel. Any dodgy business could ruin the girl's reputation in a place like Marsholm Cells.'

'Your warning is noted, Boss.'

It was some time before I had time to

speak to Nan properly. I was so busy with the alterations that I often barely looked up when she brought food for Samuel and me. She was still training girls from the village, so she often took on more than one role. In her way she was every bit as useful as Samuel, and went about her work without a fuss.

To begin with, I just looked at her long enough to see that she was a little bit older than I had thought. In her early thirties, I guessed. I could see what Samuel meant about her having something about her. She was not pretty, but she was striking. She could be brusque with the others girls, but there was kindness in her voice, and she was always fair.

She had been working for me about a month when she brought us sandwiches for our luncheon and Samuel said, 'Nan, tell the boss about Miss Hetty.'

I knew who he meant straight away. Who else could it be? For a horrible moment I thought Nan was going to say that Henrietta had died. The sadness on her face seemed to suggest it.

'I'm just worried about her, that's all,' said Nan. 'But it's nothing to concern His Grace about.'

'She is a relative,' I said, acutely aware of how little that had meant to me over the years.

'Your Grace, there's things that happened in this house that no one knows about; and now she's been taken away from us to be married, and Miss Cora has gone there, and I don't know what will happen.'

To my amazement, Nan began to cry, though she immediately checked herself. 'Oh, I'm sorry, Your Grace. I'll take myself away . . .'

'You'll do no such thing. Sit down.' I led her to a chair near the fireplace. 'Samuel, will you pour Nan a cup of tea?'

She gave me a strange look, and I think that it was then she began to trust me. I know why now. It was because Mrs Charlotte Marsh had treated her with the same kindness, and as if she were an equal.

I may have been a duke, but I hardly felt like one, so if I overstepped the boundaries of familiarity occasionally, it was perhaps to be expected. I was not used to having servants, apart from the haphazard maids my mother sometimes employed during the good times, and even though Samuel insisted on calling me Boss. I did not know that one was not supposed to sit and take tea with them.

I know it now of course, but as I am a duke of some status in life, I hardly care if it is the wrong thing to do. People forgive a lot when one has money and status, and my friendships with those who work for me is seen as eccentricity, rather than common human decency.

'Tell me all about it,' I said, when Nan had composed herself.

That was when I learned all about Henrietta and her manipulative cousin Cora. As Nan told her story, I was engulfed with the shame that because of my stupid pride, I had left Henrietta to her fate. At that time I dared not tell Nan that I had already met her Miss Hetty. It was too embarrassing.

'We must do something,' I said. 'There is something fishy about this whole situation. I do not trust Sir George Lakeham, for a start.' How much of that was genuine suspicion, or just plain old-fashioned jealousy, I do not know. 'Samuel, I want you to do some digging. Find out about the man and all the people he knows.'

'Will do, Boss.'

'What can I do?' Nan asked. 'I want to help.'

'You can come with me,' said Samuel, 'if the Boss doesn't mind. I, er . . . I need someone to write things down.'

'Good idea,' I said, at the same time casting Samuel a warning glance. I already admired Nan, and I did not want him to ruin the girl. 'Are you willing to do that, Nan?'

'Of course. I'll do anything to help her.'

'Very good.'

When Samuel and Nan's investigations led them to the south of France, I took the opportunity to go down to Lakeham Abbey. The ruinous residence was in extensive grounds, and I found out that if I stayed in the area of the lake, I could watch the house without being observed. There was a public footpath there that was used regularly by locals and tourists in the area. There was also a small island in the middle.

The first couple of times I did not see her, and I feared I never would. Then one day she came right down to the lake and rowed to the island. Her face had changed. It was no less beautiful, but it held a world-weariness that should never have appeared on the face of one so young. Yet standing there for ten minutes or more would see those cares slip away, and her face would clear. It was almost as if the visit to the lake was something of a rest cure for her.

I wanted to talk with her, but did not know how to bring that about. Then I had the idea of rowing over to the island, and hoping she would not be too horrified to see me.

That is where we stood face to face for the first time in too many years. I could hardly speak. All I knew was that all the attraction I had felt for her came flooding to the surface. She flew into my arms and I never wanted to let her go. The more we met, the more I fell in love with her. I was right about her hidden strength. She was not aware of it, but it shone from her, even in her most vulnerable state. Somehow this young woman had survived all the mind games played by her manipulative cousin.

She told me about her life and her marriage. You will forgive me, I hope, for feeling some joy in the fact that her marriage was loveless. I wanted her to love me. But she was hopelessly trapped, and until I could find a way for her to leave Lakeham Abbey without a taint on her character, she would remain trapped.

Please believe that I did not care if there was a scandal. At least not for myself. I was the son of a man who had died in a debtors' prison and an actress who had known more than her fair share of protectors over the years. I only cared for Henrietta's sake. I would not allow people to whisper about her.

I had to make her see the truth about her cousin, but I did not want to turn her against me. Finally came the breakthrough I had hoped for, and she began to realise how badly Cora had used her. But it was too late by then. Before I could save Henrietta, she was taken away to the asylum.

Testimony of Dr Douglas Mackintosh

I have had the pleasure of spending several hours in the company of Lady Henrietta Lakeham. I was called in by His Grace, the Duke of Marsholm, after the young lady was freed from an asylum run by Dr Herbert Fielding. I know of Fielding, of course. He is a quack of the lowest order and has no care for his patients.

His Grace was adamant that he did not want me to assess Lady Henrietta for a return to the asylum. He only wanted to know what her previous experience had done to her mind, and how he and their friends could best help her.

I find Lady Henrietta to be a very charming, though rather shy, young lady. It is clear from all that she has told me that, from a very young age, she has been mentally abused by certain members of her family. The abuse has been insidious in nature; and whilst she has not been cruelly treated in a physical manner — apart from events related to me by Miss Anne Bradley — there has been psychological abuse. There has also been some drug abuse, both whilst she was at Fielding's asylum and before. It is my belief that someone has been giving Lady Henrietta psychotropic drugs, which have altered her perception of reality. It has left Lady Lakeham with low self-esteem, and a sometimes nervous disposition. I have often treated soldiers who have come back from the front, and I can honestly say that Lady Lakeham's state of mind is akin to that.

Is she mad? No, I do not think so, and I believe that with love and care she will recover.

Of the crimes she fears she has committed, I have no comment to make, other than if Lady Lakeham is a murderer, then she is one of the best actresses I have ever met.

10

The Journal of Henrietta Lakeham

I am sure that I must be dreaming. In this dream, I awaken and go downstairs and find Max waiting at the breakfast table with his mother, and they both smile at me. Nan brings me my morning tea; and a kind man, Samuel, shares our smiles and asks if I am well this morning.

To make the dream even more wonderful, I am back in my own home, Marsholm Manor, only it has been modernised, and the gardens are lovingly tended again. I am back in my own bedroom, which has been redecorated with yellow daffodils on the wallpaper and gold drapes on the window, giving the room a sensation of it always being spring.

More importantly, I feel that I am

loved and cared for, for the first time since my mother and father died. Surely, I think, this dream will end and I will awaken back in the hospital, with Dr Fielding's treatments and the indifferent care of the orderlies.

But the dream continues; and after so many days of waking to the same comfortable scenes, walking out in the garden with Max, and spending after-noons listening to Celia's tales of the theatre — where she often performs some of her most fêted roles, much to my amusement — I begin to believe in the dream. I spend the evenings in my sitting room, sewing with Nan. I am healing. I am also beginning to realise that this is my real life, and everything that went before was the nightmare.

Sometimes I think they watch me carefully, only they try not to appear to do so. Nan said, 'We don't want to make you feel like a prisoner, Miss Hetty. But we're so afraid of losing you again. Until we can bring those people to justice and free you from that marriage, we won't rest.'

I hardly know what to make of Max. He is as handsome as ever, but he is also a duke, and therefore has become a very important man. The only shadow in this dream is the barrier that now comes between us. Strange that it was not there when I was married to another man; but now we are able to be together, it leaves us both feeling awkward. Me, because he is so far above me now, and him because he sees me as a broken bird to be handled with the utmost care.

Sadly, this led to an argument. It happened as we were walking in the garden one morning, and I saw the hunting lodge far in the distance. 'I would like to invite my aunts to tea,' I said, 'with your permission.'

'Hetty . . . Henrietta, how can you want to see those two old witches again?' he asked. 'After the way they took part in your torment.'

'They're just silly, lonely old women, Max. Don't you see? They will always defer to the most powerful person in the room. For so many years, that was Cora. But it does not matter. If I cannot bring them here, I will go and visit them.' I stuck my chin out. I was not used to sticking up for myself, but I felt it was about time I did.

'No,' he protested. 'What if they tell Cora they've seen you? No one is even supposed to know you're here. No, I will not allow it.'

'You will not allow it?' I felt myself becoming angry. Had I swapped one prison for another? 'Max, I am very grateful for all that you have done for me, and if we ever get my fortune back, I will repay you. But you are not my keeper, and neither are you my hus — ' I faltered. 'Molly and Dolly are the only family I have known since Mother and Father died.' I held out my hand in supplication. 'Don't you see that if I cannot forgive them, then I can never move on and be completely free?'

'Do as you will,' he said, his face darkening. 'But invite them here, where we can keep an eye on them.'

'Thank you,' I said quietly. I turned and started walking back to the house.

'Hetty . . . I don't mean to try to rule you. I have no idea what it was like for you in that place. But I do know what it was like for those of us waiting outside. I'm afraid that something might upset you and you will end up in such a place again.'

I turned back. 'Do you think I am mad?' I still doubted myself sometimes. To think that he might doubt me was like a dagger to my heart.

'No.' He shook his head. 'Not at all. But I do think you have been through a terrible ordeal, and it was one that started when you were ten years old, perhaps even younger. Molly and Dolly played their parts in that, either wittingly or otherwise. I . . . we all love you, and we will never countenance anyone undermining you or making you feel like a lesser being ever again.'

'You have to trust me, Max. Don't forget that in the past I did not know what was being done to me. Now I do.'

He nodded. 'Very well. But we'd best keep Nan away from the gun room. If those silly women say anything out of turn, she'll have at them.'

I laughed at that, and he took my hand and kissed it. 'We do not want to imprison you,' he said. 'We just want to protect you.'

'I know.'

Nan was even more against inviting Molly and Dolly to tea than Max, but despite our being friends, she still held some of the deference of a servant. We were drinking our last cup of tea of the day before I settled down to sleep. 'Well . . . ' she said when I told her. She folded up her sewing and almost threw it into the basket. 'Well, I suppose if that's what you want.'

'Nan, you're not happy about it, are you?'

'They could have protected you, but they didn't. That's all I'm saying on the matter. It's up to you.'

'They were afraid of Cora,' I said.

'Everyone was. Even you.'

'No.' Nan shook her head vehemently. 'I was not afraid of her. I was only ever afraid of her turning you against me, because then I wouldn't have been able to stay.'

'She told me that you had left me,' I said, remembering that awful day.

'I wouldn't have done that of my own accord, Miss Hetty. Never. I promised your mum I'd look after you. But when the twins dismissed me, I had no one to argue my case. You were away in Europe. I thought of writing to you, but then I thought to myself, 'At least she's away from it all now,' and I didn't want to remind you of the way things had been.'

I reached out and held her hand as tears stung my eyes. 'It's been a long, hard fight for you, hasn't it?' I asked.

'It's been even longer for you,' she said, and I could see her eyes were damp too.

'It's time to forgive, Nan,' I said. 'Not Cora. Never Cora. I promise. But

Molly and Dolly are old and alone. One day one of them will die, and the other won't know what to do on their own. I cannot find it in me to do anything other than pity them.'

'You are a much better Christian than me, Miss Hetty. That's all I can say.'

'No, Nan. No one could be that.'

'Why now?' she asked me. 'Why bring the aunts here now?'

'Because we can't stay here forever, Nan. It's good of Max — His Grace — to put us up, but eventually, if I get my fortune back, I have to live somewhere and I'll need family around me.' She scoffed when I said 'family'. 'No one's family is perfect, Nan. But I do think that without Cora's influence, we could be happy again. You . . . you will come with me, won't you? At least for a while.'

'I'm staying with you forever, Miss Hetty. Like I promised.'

'What about Samuel?'

'If he wants to be with me, he'll have

to stay as well.' She looked a little doubtful about that.

Testimony of Molly and Dolly Marsh

We had Never heard anything like it. Invited to tea with an Actress. She might have been the Mother of a Duke, but she was still on the Stage. It was Outrageous and only Proved to us how unstable Hetty was to become Friends with such a Person.

Of course we did not Refuse. It was our Christian duty to go along and let this Woman know exactly what we thought of her and her Profession. Not that We said so. We only intended to show our Disdain by remaining Silent.

We suppose Mrs Celia Marsh was Charming enough, and she had the sort of Beauty that lasts forever. 'Do come in,' she said, all Smiles. What a Pity those smiles hid such Sin. We had been pondering to each other before we Arrived as to what Nature that Sin might take. We could Hardly bear to Think about it. 'You know Miss Bradley, our housekeeper, of course. She will show you where you may freshen up.'

And there she was, Large as Life. Nan Bradley. Though we are Christians and should Forgive, we had not Forgotten her Insolence.

'Miss Molly, Miss Dolly,' she said, nodding Curtly. 'Follow me.' Hetty was nowhere to be seen at that time.

Nan led us to a room on the First Floor, which we Realised had once been Cora's bedroom. It had been Redecorated, but we cannot say that we Liked the Style. It was too Bright, and had that new Electric light, which we feel is far too Harsh on the Complexion.

We went back downstairs to the Drawing Room, where we met a Black man who offered us Sherry!

'A butler from the colonies. How Avant Garde,' one of us said.

'Samuel is not a butler,' said the

Duke. 'He is my friend. He will be joining us for dinner.'

We could see Immediately what sort of Household Marsholm had become, and we Both thanked the Lord that we no longer had to live There. Luckily we were too Well-Mannered to say anything.

Hetty Joined us soon after. We Daresay the girl was Kind enough to us. She kissed us and Hoped that we were well.

'We were just saying,' one of us Said, 'that the room in which we refreshed ourselves was Cora's bedroom. We spent many happy hours there with dear Cora, brushing her beautiful hair.'

'Yes, I remember,' said Hetty. Of course the Girl started sulking then. The duke put his Hand on her Shoulder, which was rather Familiar if you ask us.

'We don't talk of Cora in this house,' he said.

'That is most irregular,' one of us said. 'She is, after all, our kin.'

'It doesn't matter, Max,' Hetty said. She put her hand on his in a similarly Familiar manner. What can one Expect when she lives with an Actress now? 'I'm all right, really. I know that Molly and Dolly are very fond of Cora.'

'She is an Angel,' we said. 'And we do not like the way she is being vilified by certain members of this family. People have quite the wrong idea about her.'

'Then perhaps you might have checked her behaviour more often,' said the Duke, 'so that no one could have reason to get the wrong idea.'

Hetty said, 'Max, please. We won't talk about this now. For I am glad to have my family with me. Is it time for dinner yet? It must be time for dinner.'

'Of course, darling,' said Mrs Celia Marsh, putting her Arm around Hetty's shoulder. Really, the Girl would be getting too Sentimental from such overt shows of Affection. We always say that One must Not show too much Attention to Children, otherwise One will Spoil them. 'You must be hungry

221

after your walk today. I will tell the butler to hurry things up.'

In our Day, the servants were Not told to 'hurry things up'. The butler served Dinner at a Time that he deemed Appropriate, and if one wanted to change it, one had to give him Plenty of notice.

We went in to dinner, Noting that a lot of money had been spent on the Dining room. It was all Gilt and Glass and rather too bright for our Liking. That was the problem with the Lower Classes who came into riches. They always Over-did things. We knew that the Duke had only been a Shipping clerk before inheriting from Julius and the old Duke. We were quite Surprised to see that he ate not Only with the Correct cutlery, but with his Mouth closed.

'Celia,' said Hetty, 'you must tell Molly and Dolly about the time that you performed for the Prince of Wales.'

'The Prince is a profligate man,' one of us said. 'It is no honour to perform for him.' We did not read the Gossip columns ourselves, but our maid did, and we felt it our Duty to ask what she had read to Ensure that she does Not become Corrupted.

'I felt it was an honour,' said Mrs Celia Marsh, without any sense of Shame. 'We performed *Romeo and Juliet*. I played the Nurse.'

'Yes, well,' we said, 'we cannot imagine you'd be allowed to play someone of high birth.'

'You mean like Cleopatra,' said Mrs Celia Marsh, 'or Queen Elizabeth? Or Anne Boleyn? I am pleased my directors did not think as you did.'

'I've seen Celia act,' said Hetty. 'Only here, in private, but she's a wonderful actress and can play any part she sets her mind to.'

'And how would you know?' we asked. 'You did not go to plays. We were determined not to corrupt your young mind.'

'Oh, I think plays must be wonderful,' she said. 'They take us out of the ordinary and into a magical world. They also teach us to think about how we might behave in a similar situation.'

'Really, Hetty,' one of us said. 'You do not know what you are talking about. Now Cora, she has a good brain.'

'She is certainly clever,' said the duke. We were Gratified that he agreed with us, Even if he did look rather Grim as he said it.

'Have you heard from her?' the black man asked. 'Lately, I mean.'

It took us a Moment for us to realise he was Addressing us. So of course, We did Not reply. After all, how does one Speak to a Black man? He was not a Servant, so we could not speak to him as one of the Lower orders. But neither was he of noble birth, so we could not Speak to him as an Equal.

'You were asked a question,' said the duke. 'Samuel asked if you had heard from Cora.'

'No, Your Grace, we have not. At least, not since she told us she was returning to France. And is it any wonder, with the terrible things that have been said about her in this household? To think we helped to raise that poor girl, when she had no family.'

'She did have a family,' said the man called Samuel. 'You were lied to. Her father died but her mother did not.'

It was the First we had Heard of it. 'We are sure dear Cora had her reasons for lying,' we both insisted.

'She was just a child,' said Hetty, looking at the duke and Samuel, 'when she first came here.'

'We know that, dear heart,' said the duke. 'But even then she was dangerous, as Nan can testify.'

'Dangerous? Our girl, dangerous?' We were Horrified. 'She is no more dangerous than we are.'

For some reason the duke laughed at that. 'Max . . . ' his mother Chided. 'How do you like what we have done with the garden?' asked Mrs Celia Marsh.

'It is passingly good,' we agreed.

'Though in our day, we would not have had so many colours. It tends to be garish.'

'Thank you,' Mrs Celia Marsh said, looking as if she might Laugh too. 'I chose them myself.' Then she did the Strangest thing. She turned to Hetty and said, 'You poor, darling girl.' We have No idea what That was about, but it caused Hetty to get up and Run from the room, Crying.

Dinner seemed to finish Quickly after that. Mrs Celia Marsh disappeared upstairs after Hetty, and We were sent to the Drawing room whilst the duke and his exotic Friend drank their port.

Mrs Celia Marsh returned about half an hour later. 'My apologies,' she said, looking rather tight-lipped. 'I have been tending to Henrietta.'

'You spoil the girl,' we both Agreed.

'It is about time someone did,' said Mrs Celia Marsh. 'We invited you here because that darling, forgiving child asked us to. She felt some affinity with you because you share the same blood.'

She put her hand to her Forehead. 'Lord knows why. You belittle her at every opportunity. You belittle everyone. For myself, I do not care. I have been called many things during my career as an actress, some of which I may have even deserved. Though I swear that whatever I did to protect my son, I never hurt another living being. But the way you abuse that child . . . have been abusing her all her life, egged on by Cora . . . You should be ashamed of yourselves. I am going to ring the bell and ask the footman to bring your garments. Rest assured that if I have anything to do with it, you will not be welcome in this house ever again.'

'Well *really*,' we both replied in indignation.

'Yes, really,' said Mrs Celia Marsh.

'We do not have to take this from an actress.'

'Remember that I am also the mother of a duke. Whilst you may not approve of me, many in the county will. Or at least they will pretend to, because of my son's status. On the other hand, because I was not raised as nobility, I do not have to follow their rules of noblesse oblige when dealing with rudeness. You are small-minded and cruel, not to mention rude and ungrateful to people who are kind to you. Remember it was the interest from Hetty's inheritance that kept you after Julius and Charlotte died. You were happy enough to live off her money whilst you helped Cora destroy every vestige of self-esteem that child had. I don't think Miss Cora had to dig very deep to find the darkness in you two. It was ever thus, wasn't it? That need to injure others because of the hatred you have in your hearts for anyone who you feel has more than you. Hetty said she was afraid that you would end up poor, old and alone, which is why you were invited tonight. She wanted to forgive you. She is a much better person than I or anyone else could be. I think you deserve to be poor and alone.'

'Forgive us? What reason could Hetty have to forgive us? We have done nothing.'

'Yes,' said Mrs Celia Marsh. 'That is very much the problem. You have done nothing whilst that girl was tormented to the point of madness.'

We had Never been Spoken to in such a way. We left, of course. Let it not be Said that We would Stay where we were not Wanted.

We still have Friends in the district. When we make a point of Speaking to People — and by People we mean respectable folks — in Marsholm Cells, they will always reply, even if they Always seem to have to Rush off elsewhere. If we do not get as many Invitations as we used to, then it is because people Understand that we are growing Older and cannot Venture out as much.

There was a Difficult time when the duke wanted us to leave the Hunting Lodge. We gather that Hetty talked him out of it, and We suppose we Should be Grateful to her for That, if nothing else.

11

Testimony of Nan Bradley

So much has happened since the aunts came to dinner that I'd almost forgotten that awful evening. I wasn't present for the meal and only learned after, from Samuel, how painful it was. He came to get me so I could go to Miss Hetty, but Mrs Celia Marsh was already in Miss Hetty's sitting room, doing her best to soothe her.

'I'm sorry,' she kept saying to Mrs Marsh. 'I'm so sorry. I should never have invited them. I can't believe how rude they were to you. And to Samuel. I'm so ashamed of them.'

'Hush now,' Mrs Marsh said. She smiled at me as I put a cup of tea on the bedside table. 'You have no reason to feel ashamed, Hetty. You thought the best of them, which is what we must always try to do with others.'

'I had forgotten how small-minded they were,' said Miss Hetty. 'I had hoped that they had some care for me. I remember Cora saying to them that everything she did, she did for my sake. Now I realise it was so they could feel better about the way they treated me.'

Samuel knocked on the door and coughed politely before entering. 'The ladies are alone in the drawing room and the Boss doesn't feel inclined to go in and see them.'

'I will go,' said Mrs Marsh. 'I have a few things I wish to say to them.'

'Say a few things for me while you're at it,' I said. Mrs Marsh laughed at that.

All I know after that is that the ladies left much earlier than intended and they were never invited to the house again.

'I must speak to Max,' Miss Hetty said. 'I owe him an apology.' She got up and left the room.

'Was dinner as bad as she thinks?' I asked Samuel.

'Worse. They were like a couple of crows, looking to peck and pierce wherever they could. They couldn't even look me in the eye. I'm used to that, but they were really rude to Mrs Marsh; yet she treated them with nothing but civility.'

'They've always been the same. I don't think Miss Cora had to encourage them that much, to be honest. I think there was always some resentment that their father had a second family; and whilst they loved Miss Cora's father, because a second-born son he was no threat to them, they were not so keen on having to take charity off Mr Julius Marsh. Why he put up with them both, I'll never know. Probably because he was as kind as his daughter.' I sighed heavily. 'I sometimes think kindness is a curse, Samuel.'

'I disagree. I believe we should always try and think the best of people. At least until they give us reason to believe otherwise.'

'How can you say that, when you

have been treated so poorly?'

'What's the alternative, Nan? To be bitter and angry all my life?' He shook his head. 'That is not the way to move forward.'

'Is that what you think I am? Bitter and angry?'

He laughed and put his arms around me. 'You are a saint. A rather frightening one at times, and certainly not a person to have as an enemy. But you are on the side of the angels, and for that reason, I love you.' He breathed in deeply as if bracing himself for something. 'I had a letter from the Buchets this evening.'

'Oh?' We had been writing to Madame and Monsieur Buchet since we left France, and they had been keeping us up with developments from the Lakeham house. So far, there had been little news. The Lakehams appeared to be lying low. 'Why didn't you bring it to me to let me read it?'

'I wanted to practise on my own, since you've been teaching me. I think I've got the gist of it.'

'What does it say?'

'They say, amongst other things, that some grand duke is looking for someone to build a palace for him. They've given him my name.'

'That's wonderful, Samuel. But what about your work here?'

'It's almost done, and it's time I let the Boss spread his wings without me. Time I did my own thing too. I want you to come with me, Nan. Say yes.'

'What else does the letter say?' I asked, stepping away from him. I loved him, but going to France would mean leaving Miss Hetty again. She needed me more than ever, with the Marsh twins treating her so poorly.

'How did you know there was something else?'

'I can see it in your face. You're telling me the good news first.'

'Promise me first that you'll come with me.'

'I can't leave her, Samuel.'

'Not even for me?'

'I love you. More than anything.'

'No, you don't. That's the problem. You don't love me more than her.'

'Samuel, this isn't about loving her more. Not in that way, anyway. It's about keeping a promise.'

'It's time you had your own life, Nan.'

'Tell me what else it said in the letter. You're keeping it back because you know it'll make me say no, aren't you?'

He took the letter from his pocket and let me read it. The first few lines set out why Samuel knew I wouldn't leave with him.

'*We've heard that the Lakehams have packed up and left,*' wrote Madame Buchet. '*Word is that they're coming back to England. So it looks like that job has fallen through for you. But there is a grand duke who . . .*'

After that, we argued about the letter. I remember throwing it down and leaving the room in a huff. Samuel came after me, and we made up, as we always did when we argued, but I still wouldn't leave with him and couldn't make him understand why.

I went to bed late, and didn't have reason to go and see Miss Hetty until the following morning. By then it was too late. Her bed was empty, but the letter lay on top of the counterpane, along with a note.

Letter from Henrietta Lakeham

My dearest Nan,

I am sorry to leave without warning, but I know you would try to stop me. Please understand that I must face up to my tormenters. It is the only way I can put the dark past behind me.

I have not spoken about the night I was taken from Lakeham Abbey, because I was afraid of what the truth might be. Now I want to tell you the truth, in as much as I know what the truth is.

I had returned from the lake with conflicting emotions. Whilst I had admitted that I hated Cora, there was a part of me that still denied it. How could I hate my childhood friend? For it seemed to me that Cora had always been there. Except I was beginning to see that the darkness I had felt following me for all my life came from her. I finally began to realise how many times she had insulted me and undermined my feelings. How many times she had told me that others hated me, whilst declaring that she wished to say no such thing. She even did the same with you, Nan; trying to keep us apart, so that I was isolated and could only turn to her for support.

I was torn between confronting her with this truth, and with just running away. Max had not asked me to go with him, but I believed I still had some money of my own. I did not care about the scandal. It was much worse to stay in that house with three people who had no affection for me.

I went to my sitting room and the

writing table where I kept my chequebook. When I opened the drawer, I found all the cheques gone. That could not be so. I knew I had not used them all. I went to Cora's writing desk. I told myself that it was just to see if I had, for some reason, left a newer chequebook there. Deep down I knew it was because I no longer trusted her. When I opened her desk, I did not find a chequebook. But I did find a sheet of paper upon which my name was written several times, until, towards the end of the list, it became a passing facsimile of my signature.

I turned around to find Cora standing at the door. 'What have you done?' I asked.

'I am not sure what you mean, dearest.'

'I know that you have taken my cheques. I know that you have been practising my signature. What have you done?'

'You are tired, dear heart. Come

and lie down. I'll bring you a cup of tea.'

'I don't want a cup of tea, Cora. I want the truth.'

She would not be swayed. I had imagined it all, she said. 'There was no chequebook, darling. You spent all your money on your honeymoon. I knew it was foolish, but I did not like to say. You have forgotten. As you always forget these things.'

'Let us see what my husband has to say about that,' I said. I swept from the room and went in search of Sir George. I imagined that he had always been honest with me, even if he did not love me. I see now how foolish I really was.

'What Cora says is correct, Henrietta,' he said, his eyes cast to the ground. 'You spent it all on our honeymoon.'

'Fifty thousand pounds? In six months?'

'I tried to stop you, but you said you were so glad to be free of your aunts and able to do what you wanted.'

I neither remembered the conversation nor spending my money. I argued with them both to that effect. Sir George's mother became involved.

'You are just a silly, careless girl who looks to blame others for her own mistakes,' she said. 'I told George he should not have married you.' At least in that, I felt, she spoke the truth. She had always been jealous of her son. Sometimes I felt her jealousy went beyond that of a loving and overprotective mother.

The argument raged until dinnertime, with the three of them bullying me into submission. I did finally submit, but only because I was exhausted. My only means of escape — the money left to me by my mother and father — had all gone. I was trapped in a loveless marriage and living in a house that appeared to hate me as much as the people in it did.

I remember going to bed without eating dinner. Cora came to my room and tried to console me, but I

240

pushed her away. For the first time since she had come into my life, I saw that she was a viper, dripping with poisonous venom. Why had I not seen it before?

At some point, several hours later, I woke up, dehydrated from my tears, and took a drink of water. I do not remember where the water came from. It was on the bedside table, and I supposed I must have put it there.

After that, things become less certain. I think I slept a little while longer, and then I heard a scream from the chamber above me. I stumbled from my bed, and the very room seemed to lurch about me, but the screaming continued. I went upstairs and saw a tableau in front of me. Or it might have been in the mirror. There might have been a dozen mirrors, so distorted was my vision. A woman who looked like me, with hair hanging around her face — the ghost of Lakeham Abbey — stood over a body. It was Sir George's body. Once again I saw the red mist that I had seen when my mother and father died.

Cora and the Dowager Lady Lakeham were standing nearby. I heard Cora say, 'Oh, Henrietta, dearest, what have you done?'

It was then that I started screaming, and I did not stop until they took me to the asylum.

They say it was an illusion. That I did not really kill him. I just thought I had.

Now, perhaps, you understand why I must go to Lakeham Abbey. I must see for myself if he is still alive. I must know the truth. If he is dead, then I must know how he died.

Only when I know the truth can I return and start living. If the truth is that I killed him, then it must also be true that I killed my parents. In which case I shall give myself up to the police and let the law decide my fate.

I know you will be hurt that I have

gone without you, but you must understand why I cannot involve you or the duke in this. I will not bring this scandal upon the only people who have ever truly cared for me. It is better to forget me and know that I release you from my mother's promise. Samuel loves you so much. I see it in his eyes whenever he looks at you. Go with him to France. Have beautiful children and, if you can, try and remember the good things about me.

Please tell the duke that he was, and always will be, my only love. And you, dear Nan, have been my most faithful friend. In a dark world that has sometimes seemed unreal to me, my love and affection for both of you has been the only truth worth knowing.

Your friend,
Henrietta Lakeham

12

Testimony of Maximilian, Duke of Marsholm

Nan came to me as soon as she found the letter from Hetty. I struggled to put aside the hurtful fact that she had not written to me. Seeing how she declared her love for me helped heal some of that ache.

I knew that things had changed between us. It had been easier to show our feelings when she was at Lakeham Abbey. Being close together, and knowing we could not act upon our love until her marriage was over, had left us feeling constrained. But she loved me, and I was determined that at last I would become worthy of that love.

We had no idea how long Hetty had been gone. All we knew was that she had taken a horse from the stables in the early hours of the morning, which put her several hours ahead of us. Lakeham Abbey was nearly a day's ride away in fine weather, but by the time we were able to set off the skies had turned grey and rain began to fall, which made the going harder for us.

Nan insisted on accompanying us, even though Samuel and I felt she should stay behind.

'I'm coming with you and that's that,' she said. Then she remembered to curtsey. 'If it's all right with you, Your Grace.'

Samuel looked at me and shrugged, but I could see the pride in his eyes. It was amusing to see that she was more than a match for him.

As we left, my mother took my hand. 'Bring her home, Maximilian,' she said, with tears in her eyes. 'Whatever happens, bring her home. I always worried for you — that you were so idealistic, you wouldn't find the right person to love in this world. Well, you have found her, so whatever you do, don't lose her. Never mind the scandal. We can worry about that later. You could go abroad again, if necessary.'

It was a thought that had occurred to me, if it seemed that Hetty could not escape her marriage. I had hesitated to put it to her, for fear of offending her. I was past that now, knowing that she loved me. I believed that if I asked her, she would come with me. I should have asked sooner. I should have done many things sooner, and I cursed my own pride and stupidity in allowing things to get so bad.

It goes without saying that the ride to Lakeham Abbey was interminable. It was not just the longing to be there, with it seeming as if the road was longer and longer. The going became worse as the day wore on and the rain fell in torrents. The horses stumbled over mud and rocks. Our clothes became soaked, and I struggled to shake off the irritation as my damp clothes stuck to me, mixing with the sweat on my skin. The muscles in my neck were taut and painful with the strain of worrying about Hetty.

What if we were too late? What if something happened to her? They might take her back to an asylum, in which case it would be easy to get her out again, as soon as we found out where she was. But my fears went far beyond that. The nature of Julius and Charlotte Marsh's deaths had been on my mind a lot. I did not believe for one minute that Hetty had killed them. Nor did I believe it had been an outsider. If I was right, and I was sure by then that I was, then Hetty might be riding into extreme danger. Now they had all her money, there was nothing left to keep her alive. I wondered that they did not kill her before.

It was dusk when we reached Lakeham Abbey. The rain had stopped. I did not wait for permission to enter the Abbey. I just stormed my way in, closely followed by Samuel and Nan. Samuel and I carried pistols, sensing that there might be trouble.

The house appeared to be empty. We went from room to room, but could find no one, not even a servant. Nan crept upstairs, and we followed her. There was no one in the rooms on the first floor, either. Then we heard a sound from above.

'Wait,' I said when Nan went to go up the second flight of stairs. 'Let us go first.'

She looked about to argue, but instead acquiesced and let us go on ahead.

We came to a long hall that looked strangely off-balance. I could not put my finger on it, but Samuel, with his keen eye for structure, understood straight away.

'They've taken out a door,' he said. 'Every other door here corresponds to one on the lower floor. But there's a door missing from this area.' He pointed to a particular part of the wall. 'And judging by this paintwork, it's not been long since they did it.'

We went along to the next door and

opened it, finding ourselves in a long chamber used to store old furnishings and paintings. I did not know it then, but Hetty had been brought to this very room and told that it had ever been thus.

'What's that sound?' asked Nan.

It sounded like someone sobbing softly. We went deeper into the room, and behind a beaten-up wardrobe found an old woman sitting in a rocking chair. 'My room,' she whimpered. 'They've stolen my room. I can't find my way around anymore.' Her hair, which was a similar colour to Hetty's — though obviously dyed — lay around her face, coarse and bedraggled.

'Who are you?' asked Nan, kneeling down in front of her.

'I'm the ghost of Lakeham Abbey,' the old woman said. She tried to laugh, but began to cry instead. 'At least that's what they tell me to say.'

'I know that voice,' said Nan. 'We heard it at Mrs Potter's house. Do you remember, Samuel?'

'Yes, I remember. It's Mrs Potter's mother.'

'Somehow I don't think she is,' said Nan.

'Who are you really?' I asked.

'I am the Dowager Lady Lakeham.'

'Sir George's mother?' asked Nan.

'Am I? I forget now. Yes, I think I am. Only, she is too. The other one. They didn't trust me to get it right.'

'Who didn't trust you?'

'They didn't. George and his wife.'

'Henrietta?' I queried.

'Yes. No. I don't remember now. She'll be so angry with me. She'll beat me again.'

The woman lifted her head to us and by the dim light, we could see dark purple patches on her face. 'She'll beat me. And he lets her. He just stands there and lets her. My boy, who I raised.'

'Hetty beats you?' asked Nan.

'No, the other one.'

'We'll get you some help,' I promised.

'Absinthe,' said the old woman.

'Excuse me?'

'Absinthe. I want absinthe. They promised it to me if I did as they asked.'

'That's what's addled her mind,' Samuel suggested in a low murmur. He turned to the woman. 'It's all right, m'lady. We'll get you some absinthe.'

'You're a black man.'

'How can you be sure you're not hallucinating, m'lady?' asked Samuel, earning a nudge in the ribs from Nan.

'Have you seen Lady Henrietta?' I asked the old woman impatiently. 'Is she here?'

'She was. But now she's gone.'

'Do you know where?' It was a futile question, I know. After all, the woman had shown herself unable to comprehend much.

'Where she always goes. She didn't think anyone would see. But you can from here. Not that I told the others.'

'Where she always goes?' I frowned and went to the window to think it through. Where might she always go?

As I looked out in the dusk, I saw

flickering lights coming from the lake. That was what the old woman meant! She had been watching Hetty whenever she visited the lake. Even in the growing gloom, it was possible to see the clearing on the island. In the clearing, I could see a cloaked figure. I would know those elegant movements any-where. On the main bank I could see three other figures, moving towards a boat.

'She's there!' I cried, dashing from the room.

I was vaguely aware of Samuel and Nan following me, but all I could think was that Hetty was in grave danger and I had to get to her.

The boat had reached the edge of the island by the time I got there. Without thinking — and I was already soaked to the skin — I jumped into the lake and swam across. It did not occur to me then that my pistol would be rendered unusable. I just needed to get to Hetty.

I pulled myself out onto the inner bank, slipping on the wet ground. The rain had left it drenched and full of muddy holes. My clothes were not just wet by then; they were caked in mud. When the weight of my overcoat threatened to pull me down, I took it off and threw it to the ground.

As I neared the centre of the island, I could hear a smooth voice talking. 'Hetty, you're tired from the ride, darling. Let us take you inside. We've been so worried about you.'

'I want the truth,' I heard Hetty say. 'I saw him die, and yet here he is, standing before me.'

'It was a delusion, dearest.'

'Speak for yourself,' I heard Hetty say. 'Go on, you coward. Tell me why I saw you lying in a pool of blood.'

'Henrietta.' It was a man's voice, I presumed her husband's. If my pistol hadn't been soaked, I'd have liked to kill him there and then. 'As Cora says, you're very tired. You've been ill, for a very long time.'

I noticed that there was little conviction in his voice. I had lived around actors long enough to know that he sounded as if he was reading lines he had read so often he had stopped believing them.

'And her,' Hetty said. 'Who is she?'

'She's my mother, of course.'

'No!' Hetty shouted.

I had moved close enough to see the tableau clearly. Cora, Sir George, and the woman I imagined had been described as his mother stood with lanterns, watching Hetty carefully. She was in the centre, her hair almost as bedraggled as the old woman upstairs, except that Hetty had the freshness and beauty of youth on her face that gave her form a more ethereal look.

'You're lying to me,' said Hetty. 'I know you are. There's an old woman upstairs. She says that she is the Dowager Lady Lakeham. Who is this woman?' She pointed to the middle aged woman on Sir George's left. 'She's not your mother, is she? I saw it on that first day, only I dismissed it as unimportant. She's too young to be your mother. And then I realised, when I was on my way here, why she still looks familiar.' Hetty turned to Cora. 'She looks like you. All those months at the abbey and I didn't realise it. But I can see it now. Now you're both afraid of being found out.'

'Being found out for what, Hetty?' said Cora. Her voice had a harsh edge to it. 'Careful you don't get too delusional, darling. Or you may have to go back to that asylum. We can't have you imagining your lover again, can we? What was his name? Max?'

'He exists. I know he does.'

'No, dear.'

'I've been at Marsholm Manor for the past few months, Cora. I know he's real. He's the Duke of Marsholm.'

'No, dear,' Cora said again. 'Aunts Molly and Dolly told me how they found you there, going on about some duke and his actress mother. It isn't true, Hetty. None of it is. The only truth is that you're very sick.'

'Really?' I said, stepping forward at last. I had heard all I needed to hear.

'Then you must be delusional too, cousin Cora.'

She spun around to look at me, her face a mask of horror. 'I . . . ' She recovered, but not quickly enough. 'I thought I heard something. Did you hear something, Sir George? But there's no one there. She's imagining it all again.'

'He's there. I can see him,' said Hetty. 'Don't tell me that you can't.'

'No, dear, I see no one. What about you, George? Lady Lakeham?'

'Give it up, Cora,' Sir George said quietly. 'I'm tired of it all. I'm tired of tormenting this girl who has done nothing to us except make us very rich.' He turned to Hetty. 'I can see him, Henrietta. He is real. I'm sorry. I'm so sorry.' He put his head in his hands.

'Shut up!' Cora screamed, going at him like a wildcat. 'Shut up! You'll ruin everything. You idiot! I knew I couldn't trust you when you started going all soft on her. Shut up! Shut up! Shut up!' She scrambled at his face, causing deep gouges with her fingernails. The other woman — her relative, presumably — pulled her off, exhorting her to be calm.

Cora turned and ran away, towards the edge of the island. There was a boat waiting there, but she did not make it that far. Her foot slipped in the mud, and very soon the rest of her body began to follow. The mud began to swallow her up, taking her down into a deep, dark pit.

Hetty was quickest on her feet, whilst the rest of us just stood there, amazed at the scene. She ran to her cousin and grabbed her hand, trying to pull her out of the mud.

'Get my hand, Cora!' she cried. 'Hold tight and I'll pull you out!' Even then, even after everything Cora had done, Hetty showed her humanity. Rather than be grateful, however, Cora started to pull Hetty down with her. They both began to sink into the mud.

Then I reacted. I rushed to Hetty and caught her waist, pulling her from her cousin's grasp. It took some time. Like many people with madness in their veins, Cora proved to be very strong. But finally, with poor Hetty's shoulder almost coming out of its socket, I was able to pull her free. She fell into my arms, covered in mud, but very much alive.

'I hate you!' Cora cried as the mud swallowed her up. 'I've always hated you, and I'll die hating you!'

They were the last words of a madwoman. Hetty hid her head on my shoulder as Cora disappeared into the marsh.

I waited there for ten minutes, with Hetty close to me. I wanted to be sure that Cora would never return. I checked all around to ensure there was no way she could escape, but the land was such that she could not have got away.

They never did find her body.

I rowed Hetty back to the shore, not really caring how Sir George and the woman had fared. Not that I needed to worry. They had already tried to escape, leaving Cora to her fate. Samuel held them at the water's edge, his pistol aloft.

'You'd better tell us the truth,' I said to Sir George. He was in no position to argue. We all went back to the abbey.

Nan, in her usual magical way, managed to find us some blankets in which to cover ourselves. She had also found some of Hetty's clothes, left behind when Hetty was incarcerated, so made sure her charge was warm and dry before Sir George began his story. My own clothes would have to dry on my body.

We all sat in the drawing room, saying very little until Hetty returned with Nan. The woman — who we were still unsure about — stood at the window, looking back toward the lake. She did not cry, but her face was etched with deep grief. I put it down to her being fond of Cora.

'Who are you?' Nan asked her. 'You say you are the Dowager Lady Lakeham, yet the old woman upstairs makes the same claim.'

'I do not have to reply to a servant,' she said, looking at Nan blankly.

'Then reply to me,' said Hetty. 'Who are you?'

'I am Adeline Marsh, formerly Adeline Smith-Warren.'

'Aunt Adeline?' Hetty shook her head, disbelieving. 'Cora's mama? But we were told you died with Uncle Alexander.'

'My husband and I thought that your father would look upon Cora with more kindness and generosity if he thought she was a true orphan.'

'Your husband? Are you telling me that Uncle Alexander is still alive?'

'No. He's dead.'

'You remarried?'

She did not reply to that. 'We had nothing, and we thought your father would help Cora.' She looked at Hetty with bitterness in her eyes, and for the first time I saw her daughter in her. 'But he did not warm to Cora as we hoped. She was a spirited child.'

'She was a little devil,' said Nan, 'that's what she was. He didn't warm to her because she harmed Miss Hetty when no one was looking and played cruel tricks on her.'

'She was just impish, that's all,' said Adeline, but there was little conviction in her voice.

'She was evil,' Nan insisted. 'Right from when she was a little girl. There was something wicked about her. Some might call it the Marsh madness, but I don't believe that. I think some people are born wrong, and that child was.'

'She was always clever,' Adeline said, ignoring Nan. 'And we felt sure Julius would settle some money upon her. Then she could help us all. Only he didn't. He didn't even leave her anything in his will.' Adeline stared blankly out of the window. 'She was always a difficult child to love, even for me.'

'Is that why she killed him when she was sixteen?' I asked. Hetty, sitting beside me, gasped, so I took her hand in mine. 'Because she thought he'd written a will in her favour? Or because he didn't?'

'He was going to send her away to an asylum,' said Adeline. 'She had to do something. She knew that the twins wouldn't send her away. They adored her. And Henrietta was too young to make that decision. Then we came up with another plan. I didn't want to do it, but Cora insisted it was our only option.'

'Marry her off to Sir George?' Samuel said. Adeline seemed even less inclined to answer him than Nan, but he had a way about him that made people do as he said.

'Oh, what do you know of what it's like to see others with money whilst you have none? My Cora grew up like that, first with us and then with Julius and Charlotte. It eats away at you, till you'll do anything to survive.'

'I grew up in a workhouse,' said Samuel. 'I had nothing, and saw lots of people with plenty. I don't pretend I've been an angel all my life, yet I never tormented an innocent young woman, and I never took someone else's life because I didn't like that they had more than me. So please, missus, don't preach to me about what it is to be poor. You don't seem to have done too badly for yourself, living in a place like this. Obviously you have a powerful friend in Sir George.'

'I knew you didn't love me,' Hetty said to Sir George. 'I knew it was for the money, but I had no idea you hated me enough to have me incarcerated in that place.'

'I didn't!' Sir George protested. I could see him for what he was: a weak man who had been pushed into a situation he did not like. But it bothered me that Hetty seemed concerned about his love. 'It was her. All her. She pushed us and pushed us until we said yes.'

'Cora, you mean?' I asked.

'Yes.'

I laughed bitterly. 'It's convenient

that now she is dead, you lay all the blame on her.'

'Tell me what you did to me,' said Hetty. 'I need to know what was real and what wasn't.'

'She drugged you,' said Adeline. 'Some concoction that would make you disorientated. Then she'd make strange noises to unnerve you whilst you tried to sleep.'

'What about the old woman?' Hetty pressed. 'The 'ghost of Lakeham Abbey'.'

'That was a stroke of luck, you seeing her,' said Sir George. He had the grace to look sheepish. 'It played into Cora's hands. We had a devil of a time altering the room, but she drugged you then. You thought you'd slept for a day or so, but it was longer than that.'

'Then, once you had all my money?'

'We knew it wouldn't be long before you realised,' said Sir George, 'so we arranged the transfer to the asylum, and the little tableau where I died. The idea was to convince you I was dead, but to let others think you'd imagined it.'

'Why? Why not just have me locked up for murder?'

'Because he would have had to hide away abroad for even longer,' Samuel cut in. 'A murder investigation requires a dead body. Questions would have been asked. But if he could convince someone like Dr Fielding that you were delusional, he could get you locked away and no one would ever know the truth. I'll guess that's the same reason they didn't kill you off. People ask questions when a healthy young woman dies.'

'Cora said she had no friends,' said Sir George. 'We thought even you — ' He pointed to me. ' — were a figment of Hetty's imagination. We thought the drugs had addled her mind.'

'Cora was convinced that no one could ever love me,' said Hetty with a shudder.

I drew her close and whispered. 'She was wrong. I love you, and Nan loves you.'

'And I love you because they love you,' said Samuel with a grin.

'Dear God,' said Adeline. 'Do we have to listen to this?'

'I can see where your daughter got it from,' said Nan, glowering at the woman.

'I want a divorce,' Hetty said to Sir George.

'Er . . . ' He hesitated, looking at Adeline as he did so. 'That might be difficult. I don't want to go to prison. I could not survive in such a place.'

'Prison? It is not a criminal offence to get a divorce,' I said.

'It is if you're married to someone else,' said Nan.

We all looked at her. 'Oh, honestly,' she said. 'I worked it out as soon as I saw the old lady upstairs. That, and the fact that her nibs there was talking about her second husband.' She gestured to Adeline. 'She's married to him, aren't you? And you can answer me this time. I'll not be talked down to by a woman who would let her husband bigamously marry an innocent young woman!'

266

'Yes, I am George's wife,' said Adeline. 'But he can't go to prison. He can't.' Her face became cat-like, and once again I could see where her daughter got her scheming nature from. 'It'll be a scandal for you too, Your Grace, if you want to marry her, and I think you do. What will society say if you marry a girl who was illegally married to a man? She's damaged goods now.'

'You're lucky you're not a man, or I would have called you out for that,' I said, standing up. 'I don't give a damn what society thinks. I will marry Hetty and I don't care if he has to go to prison so I can do it. You see, *Lady* Lakeham, I lived most of my life without money and status, and I managed quite well. If I have to give it all up, I will survive again as I survived then. That's if you want to marry me, darling?' I turned to Hetty. 'We may have to live in exile . . .'

'Yes,' said Hetty, her beautiful face breaking into a smile. She stood up and I took her into my arms. 'Yes. I'll go anywhere with you, Max. I just never want to see this house or these people again.'

'Samuel, will you fetch the police?'

'I'm on my way, Boss.'

'I'll just go and fetch some papers,' said Sir George. 'Come with me, Adeline.'

'Don't try to make a run for it,' I warned. 'We will find you.'

They left the room together and went into the study. Samuel stood outside, near to the window, and Nan stood guard at the door.

A few minutes later we heard two shots.

13

Letters from Dr Herbert Fielding to His Grace, the Duke of Marsholm

Your Grace,
I feel I must protest about your investigation into my asylum. You clearly have no understanding of the nature of my work.
When the patient was brought to me, I took her on in good faith. I will not countenance any slander against me, so if you continue to pursue this matter, I shall fight it.
Yours,
Dr Herbert Fielding

Your Grace
Further to your last letter — yes, I am aware that the patient's name was Henrietta Marsh, formerly Lady Henrietta Lakeham. I do not see why

you need to point this out.

I hope you are aware that you have ruined me.

Who, I ask, shall take care of the gentlewomen of England?

Yours,
Dr Herbert Fielding

Your Grace,

I did not take advantage of the gentlewomen of England, despite several lawsuits to the contrary.

This is what happens when a man, as is his Christian duty, tries to help people. Is it not enough that most of my staff was imprisoned for brutality, thanks to your investigation?

My clinic has been closed down by the authorities and I am being forced to go abroad.

I bid you good riddance!

Yours,
Dr Herbert Fielding

The Journal of Henrietta, Duchess of Marsholm

Two years have passed since the deaths of Cora, Sir George, and the real Lady Lakeham. My aunts, Molly and Dolly, died within a few hours of each other last year. I had not seen them for some time, and I cannot say that my life was worse for that. Yet there is still a part of me that pities them. I cannot help but think that if they had been encouraged to embrace society more as young women, they might have been very different.

My husband and I, along with his mother, live quietly at Marsholm Manor. Max knocked down the old hunting lodge and has built a bright new pavilion in its place, where we spend long summer days relaxing and having picnics.

It is a pleasure to go into the village and speak to people. We are invited to many functions, and for the first time in my life I have close female friends of my own age. It has not been easy for me. I hardly knew how to talk to them at first, but they are warm-hearted and kind young ladies, and my story is known. In fact, I learned that my story has been known for some years, with neighbours unsure how to help me without Cora and my aunts interfering.

It is an odd thing to find out that what I had thought was a dark secret is widely known. It has the effect of letting light into the dim corners that have haunted my life. I had thought I was alone, and in many ways I was, but it seems now that I was not without empathy from others who knew of my plight.

My husband has been my saviour, and he says, rather kindly I think, that I have been his. My mother-in-law is as loving as any mother could be, and she fusses over me, but not in the same cloying way as my aunts and Cora used to.

Lately, however, both have fussed even more.

As I look down at my darling twins, Julius and Charlotte, lying asleep in their cribs, I can hardly believe I have been so blessed as to find so much love in a life that, for so long, was lacking.

Not that I have forgotten the love and loyalty shown to me by Nan. My only sadness — which is mixed with pride — is that she and her husband, Samuel, are not closer to us. We visit them sometimes, and it is wonderful to see them prosper.

I would like to say that the darkness has completely gone from my life, but the past casts a long shadow, and it would be unrealistic for me to have recovered so soon from the events of my early years. I still see Dr Mackintosh occasionally, and he has done much to help me step out of the shadows.

But sometimes, late at night, I am sure I see Cora's face at the window. She is wet and bedraggled, and presses her face against the glass. An outsider looking in. Which, I suppose, is what she always was. I am sorry for her in that respect, even though she was unkind to me. I think that in the end, she was unhappier than I was. Yet, when I think I see her, I still shudder uncontrollably, afraid that she has come to swallow me up in darkness again.

Then Max is there, by my side. 'It's just a shadow, darling,' he'll say. He takes me into his arms and, with his kisses, he chases all the darkness away.

Final testimony of Nan Cooper (nee Bradley)

It's strange that you don't realise how trapped you are, until you escape. I wouldn't change the past twenty-odd years for anything. I loved Miss Hetty when she was a toddler, and I love her now. I'm glad of my part in keeping her safe, even if I couldn't stop everything that happened.

Then again, I hadn't realised how deep a burden I carried, until I was able to set it down. Perhaps Mrs Marsh shouldn't have asked me to watch over her child when I was little more than a child myself. But I can't regret it, as difficult as the years were.

It was hard to let go and move away with Samuel, but the truth is that I found someone I love more than Miss Hetty. I hope whoever is reading this can understand that. I know that she does.

We live well in the south of France, Samuel and I. We have bought Mrs Buchet's café from her. I run it whilst Samuel builds houses for the rich expats. For the first time I can live a life dedicated to my own needs and desires. It's not always easy to remember that. The mantle of a servant is a difficult one to remove. But as I sit here, overlooking the sea with my beautiful son in my arms, all my cares and worries drift away on the tide.

I pray to God that the end of this story is a happy one, for all of us.

We do hope that you have enjoyed reading this large print book.

Did you know that all of our titles are available for purchase?

We publish a wide range of high quality large print books including:
Romances, Mysteries, Classics General Fiction Non Fiction and Westerns

Special interest titles available in large print are:
The Little Oxford Dictionary Music Book, Song Book Hymn Book, Service Book

Also available from us courtesy of Oxford University Press:
Young Readers' Dictionary (large print edition) Young Readers' Thesaurus (large print edition)

For further information or a free brochure, please contact us at:
Ulverscroft Large Print Books Ltd., The Green, Bradgate Road, Anstey, Leicester, LE7 7FU, England. Tel: (00 44) **0116 236 4325 Fax:** (00 44) **0116 234 0205**

FINDING HER PERFECT FAMILY

Carol MacLean

Fleeing as far as she can from an unhappy home life, Amelia Knight arrives at the tropical island of Trinita to work as a nanny at the Grenville estate. As she battles insects and tropical heat, she must also fight her increasing attraction to baby Lucio's widowed father, Leo Grenville — a man whose heart has been broken, and thus is determined never to love again. Amelia must conquer stormy weather and reveal a desperate secret before she can find her perfect family to love forever.

THE SAPPHIRE

Fay Cunningham

Cass, a talented jeweller, wants a quiet life after having helped to solve a murder case. But life is anything but dull while she lives with her mother, an eccentric witch with a penchant for attracting trouble. Now Cass's father, who left the family when she was five, is back on the scene — as well handsome detective Noel Raven, with whom Cass has an electrifying relationship. As dangers both worldly and paranormal threaten Cass and those she loves, will they be strong enough to stand together and prevail?

TROUBLE IN PARADISE

Susan Udy

When Kat's mother, Ruth, tells her that her home and shop are under threat of demolition from wealthy developer Sylvester Jordan, Kat resolves to support her struggle to stay put. So when a mysterious vandal begins to target the shop, Sylvester — or someone in his employ — is their chief suspect. However, Sylvester is also offering Kat opportunities that will support her struggling catering business — and, worst of all, she finds that the attraction she felt to him in her school days is still very much alive . . .

LAURA'S LEGACY

Valerie Holmes

Laura Pennington is the wilful daughter of self-made man Obadiah Pennington. Having risen from being a humble fisherman's daughter, she is still adjusting to her new position in society. Then fate crosses her path in the person of Mr Daniel Tranton, who catches her trespassing on private land. Together they come to the aid of a young lad who has run away from servitude at a local mill. Neither realises that the men hunting him are also set on hurting Daniel. The future depends on Laura's quick thinking and actions . . .

ALTERED IMAGES

Louise Armstrong

When Cherry Hawthorn is told her image isn't right to promote the television show she invented, she decides to have a makeover. Thrilled when her dishy boss Alan Jenkins not only approves, but also promises to take the new her on a date, she sets off to Sea View Spa. There, she meets the friendly, scruffy, eccentric Edward Cameron, who immediately takes a shine to her. But can this bear of a man compete with Alan's smooth charm?